THE DOUBLE LIFE IS TWICE AS GOOD

JONATHAN AMES

Scribner
New York   London   Toronto   Sydney

SCRIBNER
A Division of Simon & Schuster, Inc.
1230 Avenue of the Americas
New York, NY 10020

First Scribner trade paperback edition July 2009

SCRIBNER and design are registered trademarks of The Gale Group, Inc., used under license by Simon & Schuster, Inc., the publisher of this work.

For information about special discounts for bulk purchases, please contact Simon & Schuster Special Sales at 1-866-506-1949 or business@simonandschuster.com.

The Simon & Schuster Speakers Bureau can bring authors to your live event. For more information or to book an event contact the Simon & Schuster Speakers Bureau at 1-866-248-3049 or visit our website at www.simonspeakers.com.

Designed by Carla Jayne Jones

Manufactured in the United States of America

10 9 8 7 6 5 4 3 2 1

Library of Congress Control Number: 2009008553

ISBN 978-1-4391-0233-6
ISBN 978-1-4391-1747-7 (ebook)

Cartoons/drawings by Dean Haspiel, pages 143, 151, 158, 160
Boxing photos by Dennis Kleiman, pages 172, 173
Elf photo by Martin Fishman, page 153
Illustrations by Nick Bertozzi, pages 208–213

For Ray Pitt

Table of Contents

SHORT STORIES

BORED TO DEATH

The trouble happened because I was bored. At the time, I was twenty-eight days sober. I was spending my nights playing Internet backgammon. I should have been going to AA meetings, but I wasn't.

I had been going to AA meetings for twenty years, ever since college. I like AA meetings. My problem is that I'm a periodic alcoholic, even with going to AA. Every few years, I try drinking again. Or, rather, drinking tries me. It tries me on for size and finds out I don't fit and throws me to the ground. And so I go crawling back to AA. Or at least I should. This last go-round, I was skipping meetings and just staying home and, like I said, playing Internet backgammon.

I was also reading a lot of crime fiction and private detective fiction, writers like Hammett, Goodis, Chandler, Thompson. The usual suspects, as it were. Since my own life was so dull, I needed the charge that came from their books—the danger, the violence, the despair.

So that's all I was doing—reading and playing backgammon. I can afford such a lifestyle because I'm a writer. I'm not a hugely successful writer, but I'm my own boss. I've written six books—three novels and three essay collections—and at the time of the trouble I had roughly six thousand dollars in the bank, which is a lot for me. I also had a few checks for movie work coming in down the road.

By my economic standards it was a flush time. I had even paid my taxes early, at the end of March—it was now mid-April—and I was just trying to stay sober and keep a low profile in my own little life. I wasn't doing any writing, because, well, I didn't have anything to say.

Overall, I was being pretty reclusive. I only talked to a few people, primarily my parents, who are retired and live in Florida and who call me every day. They're a bit needy, my senior citizen parents, but I don't mind, life is short, so if I can give them a little solace with a daily call, what the hell. My father is eighty-two and my mother is seventy-five. I have to love them now as best I can. And the only other two people I really spoke to were the two close friends I have, one who lives here in New York and the other who's in Los Angeles. I have a lot of acquaintances, but I've never had a lot of friends.

One night a week, I did leave the apartment to go see this girl. It was nice. I guess you could say that she was a friend, too, but I've never really thought of the women in my life as friends, which must be a flaw. Her name was Marie and we would have dinner, maybe go to a movie, and then we'd get into bed at her place, never my place, and the sex with her was good. But it wasn't anything serious. She was twenty-six and I'm forty-two, and I retired from being serious with women a few years ago. Somebody always got hurt, usually the girl, and I couldn't take it anymore.

Well, I'll shut up now about all this. It's not my drinking problem or my finances or my dead love life that I want to talk about. I only mention all this as some kind of way to explain why I had too much free time on my hands, because what's really on my mind is this trouble I got into because, as I said, I was bored. Bored with backgammon and bored with reading and bored with being sober and bored with myself and bored with being alive.

I should make it clear that I wasn't at all bored by the books I was tearing through and loving, but bored by the fact that I wasn't actually doing anything, just reading, though it was, in fact, Hammett and Goodis and Chandler and Thompson who sort of provoked me to take action, and it's when I took action, because of those authors' books, that I blew up my life.

It was a fantasy, a crazed notion, but I got it into my head that I wanted to play at being a private detective. I wanted to help somebody. I wanted to be brave. I wanted to have an adventure. And it's pathetic, but what did I do? I put an ad on craigslist in the "services" section under "legal." It read as follows:

Private Detective for Hire

Reply to: serv-261446940@craigslist.org
Date: 2007–04–13, 8:31AM EST

Specializing: Missing Persons, Domestic Issues.
I'm not licensed, but maybe I'm someone who can help
you. My fee is reasonable.
Call 347-555-1042

There were two other private-detective ads on craigslist and they offered all sorts of help—surveillance, undercover work, background checks, video and still photography, business investigations, missing persons, domestic issues, and two things that I didn't quite grasp—"skip tracing" and "witness locates."

I figured the only thing I could help with was trying to find someone or maybe following someone, which would most likely be a "domestic issue"—an unfaithful spouse or boyfriend or girlfriend. I didn't have any qualms about that, following an unfaithful lover, though in all the private-detective fiction I've read the heroes never do "marriage work," as if it's beneath them, but I thought it would be fun to follow somebody and to do so for the purposes of a real mission. Sometimes, probably because I want everything to be like it is in a book or a movie, I have followed people on the streets of New York, pretending I was a detective or a spy.

I did try to cover myself legally by writing in my ad that I wasn't licensed. I don't know who does license private detectives, but I figured it was a difficult process and, anyway, I just wanted to put the ad up, mostly as a lark, a playing-out of a dream, like when I would shadow people on the streets. But I really didn't think anybody would actually call me—I was offering far fewer services than the other private detectives and I was acknowledging in the ad that I wasn't exactly a professional.

If somebody did call, then I figured after talking to me they would try somebody more reputable, but whatever came of it, even if nobody called, I thought it might be something I could write about, a comedic essay—"My Failed Attempt at Being a Private Detective." Often during my writing career, mostly for my essays, I've put myself in weird positions and then milked it for humor. This situation would be like the time I tried to go to an orgy but wasn't allowed in. Even when nothing happens, you can sometimes make a good story out of it.

Anyway, I got a thrill at posting the ad, but it was a short-lived thrill. For the first day, I would go and look at my ad, admiring my own handiwork, laughing to myself, wondering if something might happen, almost as if I checked it out enough times, other people would. But then, after about a day, the thrill wore off. It was one more ridiculous thing in a ridiculous life, and, of course, no one called.

So I went back to the usual routine—I started a David Goodis novel, *Black Friday,* and once again I was spending hours playing backgammon. Then on Thursday, April 19, when I was in the midst of a good game, my cell phone rang around four o'clock in the afternoon. The number had an area code I couldn't immediately place—215. I answered the phone and kept on playing.

"Hello?" I said.

"I saw your ad," said a girl's voice.

"What? What ad?" I said. I had forgotten completely about my craigslist posting. It had been six days.

"Craigslist? Missing persons?"

"Yes, of course, I'm sorry," I said, quickly rallying, remembering my little experiment. "I was distracted. I'm sorry. And most of my clients are word-of-mouth, so I forgot about my ad on craigslist. How can I help you?"

Right away, I was trying to sound professional, and the lie about the other clients just came to me naturally. I've always been a good liar.

"It's about my sister . . ." she started to say, then hesitated, and I glanced at my laptop, at the game. If I resigned, which is the same thing as losing and at the moment I was ahead, my ranking would go down, and I hate for my ranking to go down. I've worked very hard to get it to the second-highest level. I was momentarily conflicted, but I clicked a button and resigned from the game so that I could give my full attention to this other game, this one with the young-sounding girl on the phone.

"Your sister?" I said, prompting her.

"Well, I came in from Philadelphia this morning"—she started slow and then her speech came fast, real fast, the way young girls talk—"and we're supposed to go to a show tonight. I know it's weird but we got tickets to *Beauty and the Beast*, we saw it when we were really young and loved it and now it's closing, so that's why we want to see it, but she didn't answer her phone all day yesterday or this morning, but I came in anyway, it was our plan, I figured she's just not picking up or it's not charged, she always forgets to charge her phone, but she's still not answering and now her voice mail is full, and no one at her dorm has seen her for a while and the guard let me in, but she's not in her room, the door is locked, she has a single, and I don't want to call my parents and freak them out, but I have a weird feeling, she's got this sleazy boyfriend, and I don't know what to do, and I'm at this Internet café and I always use craigslist for everything, so I typed in 'missing persons' and found you."

This was a lot to digest. I tried to break it down.

"Your sister lives in a dorm? Where?"

"Twelfth Street and Third Avenue. It's an NYU dorm."

"And where are you?" I asked.

"This café. On Second Avenue. I don't know the cross street, let me look out the window . . . Third Street."

"What's your name?"

"Rachel."

"Last name?"

"Weiss."

"Your sister's name?"

"Lisa . . . Weiss."

"And I'm Jonathan . . . Spencer, by the way . . . You can call me Jonathan. And you live in Philadelphia?" The lies were coming fast and easy. Spencer was my strange middle name. I'm Jewish but my parents loaded me up with a WASP assembly of names, Jonathan Spencer Ames.

"Yeah, I go to Temple," she said. "I'm a freshman."

"What year is your sister?"

"Junior."

"And where are your parents?"

"Maryland . . . Can you help me? I don't have anywhere to stay tonight, if I can't find her, and she has the tickets to *Beauty and the Beast*, and so I think I should just go back to Philly but I'm not sure what to do."

"I think I can help you. I can come meet you in about thirty minutes. I'm in Brooklyn, but it's a very quick subway ride. I know the café you are in . . . I charge one hundred dollars a day, but I bet I can find her by tonight or at least tomorrow. Can you afford a down payment of at least one hundred dollars to cover the first day?"

"Yes," she said. "I have money. I can go to an ATM."

"Just wait at the café. I'll be there in thirty minutes. Maybe twenty . . . What do you look like?"

"Why?"

"So I can recognize you."

"Oh . . . I have dark hair, almost black. Kind of long. I'm wear-ing a yellow dress and a kind of thick white sweater."

"Okay . . . I'll have a tan cap on. Not to frighten you, but my most distinctive feature is my white eyebrows. I'm not an albino. The sun has bleached them over the years. I'll be there by four thirty."

"I guess so," she said, a bit nonsensically. Her voice was practically a whisper. She wasn't sure she was doing the right thing. I cursed myself for possibly blowing it with the mention of the white eyebrows and sounding like a nut.

"Everything will be okay. I'll find your sister," I said.

"All right," she said meekly.

"See you in a little bit," I said, and hung up, before she changed her mind.

I put on a tie, loosened it at the collar, and undid the top button to give myself a rumpled, world-weary private-detective look, and I threw on my gray-tweed Brooks Brothers sport coat, since there was a slight chill in the air. Also, on all the covers of my Chandler novels, Philip Marlowe, the great private detective, is always wearing a sport coat. Then, so the girl would recognize me, I put on my cap, and I usually wear a hat of some kind, anyway, since I'm bald and buzz my hair down, and without hair it's a very drafty world. I was already wearing my favorite olive green corduroy pants and looking at myself in the mirror, I felt, overall, quite capable of finding this missing NYU coed, at least wardrobe-wise.

I grabbed *Black Friday* to read in the subway and was out of the apartment within five minutes of hanging up the phone.

The café had uncomfortable aluminum chairs and we sat with our legs practically touching. She was a cute little thing—very white skin and very dark hair. Her mind was soft, though, and that cut down the attraction and made it easier to keep my attention focused on the business at hand. I got the following information out of her, expanding on what she had told me on the phone: the sister, Lisa, about a year ago, had disappeared for a week with an older boyfriend (early thirties) and the family had gone into a panic; now she had a different boyfriend, but the same genus—thirtysomething, guitarist in a rock band, a bartender, and possibly a junkie; Rachel didn't want to get the parents or the police or NYU security involved, because it was probably nothing and her sister would kill her if she blew the whistle; at the same time, she had a bad feeling—she was worried that her sister had maybe starting using heroin.

I figured the boyfriend was the key to this whole thing and she told me his name was Vincent, but she didn't have a last name. He worked at a bar called Lakes on Avenue B. Rachel, on an earlier trip to the city, had gone there with her sister. The NYU students liked it because the place was lax when it came to asking for proof of age.

"Do you have a picture of Lisa?" I asked.

"No," she said. Then she remembered that her sister had sent a picture of herself with Vincent to her cell phone. From Vincent's cell phone. This was a coup—I had a picture and a number to work with. She showed me the picture—Lisa was more severe than her sister, high cheekbones, a sensual mouth, but the same dark hair and marble white skin. Vincent had a yellow, long face, a tattoo of some kind on his neck, and a false look of rock-band confidence in his eyes.

I called Vincent's number and his voice mail, like Lisa's, was full. But at least I had a number. I suggested to Rachel that we go over to Kinko's on Astor Place and that she e-mail me the picture and we print it up.

But first we called the sister, on the off chance that this could be solved right here and now and the two girls could go see *Beauty and the Beast* as planned and live happily ever after. Not unexpectedly, the call went right to the filled-up voice mail. So then we swung by the dorm, with the same hope of an easy resolution, but the sister still wasn't in her room. I instructed Rachel to ask the guard in an offhand way if he had seen her sister—she showed him the cell phone picture—and he said he hadn't.

It was now almost five thirty and as we walked over to

Kinko's, I said, giving her an out and giving me an out, "Are you really sure you don't want to go to the cops or let your parents know?"

"I'm sure," she said. "Lisa'll go ballistic. She's probably forgot about the play and is just having sex for hours. Somebody told me that if you do heroin you just keep having sex and don't want to stop."

"I think that's crystal meth," I said, "but I could be wrong." My problems have always been with alcohol and cocaine, so I wasn't too sure about these other drugs.

"Whatever," she said. "I don't even like beer. She always goes with the worst guys possible. He's either shooting her up with heroin or giving her crystal meth. It's like it turns her on to find a serial killer or something."

We stopped at the Chase Bank on Astor Place and she gave me one hundred dollars. At Kinko's, I printed up a blurry but recognizable portrait of the two lovebirds.

At Fourth Avenue, we waited for a cab to take her to Penn Station and from there she'd catch the next train to Philly.

"Are you really a professional?" she asked.

"I'm not licensed," I said, "but I've been at this a while." I had been reading pulp fiction off and on for years. It was an apprenticeship of sorts and was the little bit of truth that made the lie sound sincere. I may have been having a bipolar episode. "The first thing I'm going to do is find Vincent and when I find Vincent, I'll find your sister."

She got in a cab and as I closed the door, I said, "I'll call you later tonight."

"Okay," she said, and she looked scared and dumb. But she was a sweet kid. The cab drove off and the six o'clock light was beautiful, day darkening into night.

I stood on the corner and called information and got the number for Lakes Bar.

"Lakes." It was a woman's voice, young-sounding. I could hear a jukebox in the background.

"Is Vincent there?" I asked. "The bartender."

"He comes in after me, at eight," she said. "Works eight to four."

"Okay, thanks ... Listen, I owe him some money and I'm going to bring him by a check. Can you spell his last name for me?"

"What? Yeah. I know. It's a weird name. I'm pretty sure there are two *t*'s. E-T-T-I-N."

"Thanks so much," I said, and hung up.

People will give you anything if you just ask directly. I called information and there was only one Vincent Ettin listed in Manhattan, and this Ettin still had a landline and lived at 425 West Forty-seventh Street. I had two hours to kill before he was to be at work at eight. Maybe I could find him beforehand, so I called the number and got an answering machine. It was a no-nonsense message: "This is Vincent. You know what to do." It could have been the guy in the picture or some other Vincent Ettin. I didn't leave a message.

I walked over to West Eighth Street and took the A train up to Forty-second Street. When I got out of the subway the last of the light was gone and it was evening; 425 was an old five-story walk-up. Apartment 4F had the name Ettin next to the buzzer. I buzzed 4F. Nothing. I buzzed 2F. A voice, that of an old lady, came through the intercom: "Who is it?"

"Building inspector, let me in."

"Who?"

"City building inspector, fire codes, let me in."

The door buzzed open. I went up to the fourth floor. I knocked at 4F. No answer. I knocked again. Silence. Out of instinct I didn't know I had, I tried the doorknob and the place was unlocked. Heart pounding with the feeling of transgression, I stepped in, the lights were on, and I called out "Hello," like a fool, and then I got hit by a bad smell. There were two large mounds of shit on the floor, right near the door, and I nearly stepped on them. There was also a pool of piss, which I *had* stepped in. *What the hell is this?* I thought. I closed the door and again called out, "Hello?"

I stepped over the shit and the piss, and separate from those two grosser elements it was definitely a ragged dump of a place and reminded me of my own apartment. There was a futon couch with white hairs all over it, an old TV, a good-looking stereo, a cluttered coffee table, and at the far end a miniature, nasty New York kitchen. There were no pictures anywhere, so I had no idea if this was the apartment of the Vincent Ettin that I was looking for.

A little black-and-white mutt came from some back room off the kitchen, probably the bedroom. Its tail was between its legs and it looked defeated and humiliated. Not much of a watchdog, it came over to me and I petted its head. I went through the kitchen and looked in the bedroom—nobody was there, just an unmade futon bed, and a lot of musical equipment, several amps and three guitars, all of it new and expensive-looking. The bathroom, which was off the bedroom, was a squalid closet and also empty of human life.

The dog was following me around and I got the idea that if he hadn't been walked for a while, at least two days for the two dumps, he also probably hadn't been fed. I found a bowl and dry dog food in the kitchen and set him up. Then I headed for the front door and I noticed two things—the window behind the futon-couch was wide-open with no screen and it led to a fire escape, which would make the place pretty vulnerable to a break-in, though the unlocked door made things even easier, and I also saw that there was a cell phone on the coffee table.

The musical equipment had pretty much convinced me that this was the V. Ettin I was looking for, but then to confirm it I called the cell number I had for him and the phone on the coffee table vibrated but didn't ring. The dog looked up but then kept on eating, and the phone moving on the coffee table, like a living thing, gave me a spooked feeling. So I hung up my phone, but Ettin's phone, because of some delay in the system, still shuddered, like something twitching before dying, until it finally did stop. Then I got the hell out of there.

I took the train back downtown and then made the long walk east over to Avenue B. By the time I got to Lakes, which was at the corner of Eleventh, it was eight thirty. It was a dark, stripped-down place. It had a scarred wood bar, plenty of booze, three taps for beer, stools, some booths, and a jukebox. It wasn't too crowded, and there was a man behind the bar but it wasn't Ettin. This fellow was short and very skinny and had a shiny, shaved head. My head is shaved but I always leave it stubbly, using old-fashioned barber's clippers. This guy went at his head with a razor.

I took a stool and for a moment I thought of ordering a beer. I wavered, then regained the old sober thinking, and when the bartender came over to me, I ordered a club soda. I gave him three bucks, sipped my drink, and he took care of some other customers. I wondered if Ettin was running late or wasn't going to show up. I waited a few minutes, then I waved the bartender over, deciding to show him my full hand. I took out the picture of Lisa Weiss and Vincent Ettin, which I'd folded up and put in the Goodis novel.

"Do you know these two?"

"Yeah," he said, wary. "What's this about?"

"What are their names?"

"That's Vincent and Lisa. What the fuck is going on?"

"I've been hired by Lisa's family to find her. She's been missing for a few days and she doesn't answer her phone and neither does Vincent. Do you know where they might be?"

The bartender looked at me and then looked down the bar and out the window by the front door, not for any real reason except to avoid my eye. I took forty dollars out of my wallet and put it on the bar. I don't know who I thought I was, but I had all the moves. Shiny-head saw the money.

"Tell me what you know," I said.

"Lisa is missing?"

"Yes, and her family is very concerned."

"Well . . . okay, I don't know where she is. Vince was supposed to work tonight but he called me a few hours ago and asked me to cover for him. He said he was upstate, that his band had a gig in Buffalo."

"Buffalo?"

"That's what he said. But my phone has caller ID and it said that he was calling from the Senton Hotel and it was a 212 number, Manhattan."

"What do you think he's doing at the Senton?"

"He might be on a run."

"Drugs?"

"Yeah. He was on methadone but he went off about a month ago. First he was just snorting lines and then he started shooting it again."

Shiny realized that maybe he was saying too much, he was a natural gossip and hadn't been able to help himself. I pushed the forty over to him.

"I appreciate the information," I said.

"I'm only telling you all this because of Lisa. She's a young kid." He looked down at the forty bucks, which he still hadn't touched.

"I hear you," I said.

"What are you going to do?" he asked.

"Go to the Senton. That's probably where Lisa is."

I sat up from the stool. Shiny pocketed the forty and said, "Listen, before you came in another guy was looking for Vincent and gave me his card to give to Vincent. You'll probably see him before I do, so here's the card."

He pulled the card out of his pocket and handed it to me. On the card was the letter *G* in the middle and a 917 number. Below the number, handwritten, was *4/20/2007*, which would be the next day.

"So you didn't know this guy?"

"No."

"What was he like?"

"Spanish. A tough guy. About your height, six foot, but he looked like he lifted weights."

"How old?"

"My age. Thirties. To be honest, he kind of scared me."

I went outside, got the Senton's number, and called. They had no Vincent Ettin registered, but that didn't mean anything. I knew the Senton. It was on Twenty-eighth Street and Broadway and it was a flop hotel. Unless they were stupid, people didn't give their real names when they registered. You only went to the Senton to do drugs and hide out with prostitutes. It was run, like most flop hotels, by Indians. I knew the place because in the mid-nineties I had a booze and coke relapse and holed up there myself for two days with a prostitute. For some reason, you never want to do such things in your own home. Better to go on a run in an anonymous hotel room, and then when it's over you walk away and don't have to clean up the mess. I figured if the Senton was still in business, it probably hadn't changed much.

I got a taxi and in the ride over to the hotel, I tried Lisa Weiss's number for the hell of it and got her filled-up voice mail. I called both of Vincent Ettin's numbers, just in case he had returned to Forty-seventh Street, but no luck on that end. I thought of that sweet dog alone in the apartment. It had nice eyes.

The Senton hadn't changed and neither had that stretch of Twenty-eighth Street. All of Manhattan is being turned into one big glossy, high-end mall, but Twenty-eighth Street was still a dark and empty corridor, at least at night, and had an illicit feeling to it that was kind of comforting, like you couldn't drain all the life out of New York, even if that life was the kind that was trying to kill itself.

The Senton was just as I remembered it. It didn't have much in the way of a lobby, more of a narrow hallway, with a small alcove off to the right with one old stuffed chair and at the end of the hallway there was an Indian in an office, behind a thick bulletproof piece of glass, with an opening at the bottom of the glass for the passing back and forth of money and keys. Past the office was the beat-up-looking door to the elevator.

I approached the office and the Indian, a pockmarked, exhausted-looking fellow, said he hadn't seen the two people in the picture, which I held up to the glass, but even if he had I don't think he would have told me. I asked him if I could wait in the alcove in case they were in the hotel and I could talk to them if and when they headed out. I explained to him that I very much needed to find them, the young girl in particular.

"You could wait there, if you rent a room," he said. "It's sixty dollars for three hours, ninety for the night."

I thought of just staking out the place from the sidewalk, but I didn't know how long I would be out there and it was a bit cold, even for an April night. I decided to rent the room for three hours, see if I got lucky. Between my tip for Shiny back at the bar, not to mention the subway rides and the cab, I was losing money on this deal, not that I was in it for the money, but still. I kicked myself for not telling Rachel that there would be expenses. What had I been thinking? Marlowe always quoted a day rate *plus expenses*.

Anyway, I registered as Philip Marlowe and got the key to my room but I didn't go up to it. I went and sat in the alcove. If Vincent and Lisa headed out to get something to eat or go for cigarettes, I would be right there. I took out my Goodis novel and started reading, looking up from the page every few minutes when somebody walked past me, which meant I was eyeballing a variety of prostitutes—females, trannies, gay hustlers—and the usual ragged assortment of middle-aged married johns, plus other sundry types who were using the Senton just to party.

I read for about an hour, and then I put the book down and kind of meditated, mulling things over, trying to make sense of it—Lisa, the pretty girl in the picture with the dark hair and beautiful mouth; Vincent's empty apartment with the dog shit and the left-behind cell phone and the open window and the unlocked door; and this card from "G" with tomorrow's date written on it. In the midst of all this cogitating, my parents called. My mother had taken a t'ai chi class for seniors at the Y and my father's ring finger had bent in and he couldn't straighten it out.

We eventually rang off, and I thought some more about my "case." I didn't know what to make of anything, but in my own sick way I was having a good time. Then around eleven p.m., after sitting there for nearly two hours, I really had to go to the bathroom. I wasn't sure what to do about this. I couldn't recall Marlowe or Hammett's detective, the Continental Op, having to give up a stakeout position because of the toilet. What if during the time I was in the bathroom, I missed the two I was looking for? That would be bad luck, and from playing backgammon, I know that you get a lot of bad luck when you play a game. Mostly I had been rolling good—Ettin being listed and the door not being locked at his apartment, the bartender having caller ID and being willing to feed me plenty of information. So it was all the more reason why something should go against me.

I went back to the Indian behind the glass. I asked him if there was a toilet on the ground floor that I could use.

"No," he said. "You have a toilet in your room."

"All right, listen," I said, and I took the picture back out and again pressed it to the glass, "if these two come out while I'm in the bathroom, tell them there's someone here that needs to see them. Stall them for me."

"Fuck you," he said, but it wasn't a "fuck you" with malice. It was primarily a simple statement of refusal. It was vulgar, but there was room for negotiation.

I took twenty dollars out of my wallet and slid it through the movie-ticket opening at the bottom of the glass. He took the money and didn't say anything, but I thought he would do what I had asked.

I walked quickly over to the elevator, waited a good long time for it—and I really needed to piss—and then I rode the thing at a glacial speed up to my room on the fifth floor. The room was clean enough, cigarette burns on most every surface, but the bed was made and there was one towel in the bathroom. I took a piss and felt profound relief. Sometimes a good piss is incredible.

I took the elevator back down, again waiting at least three minutes for it, and returned to the lobby. I had been gone about ten minutes, mostly because of the elevator. I went up to the glass. "You didn't see them, did you?"

"I saw the man," he said. "He came in right after you left and went up to his room."

"Shit. Came in? You mean, he didn't go out? And the girl wasn't with him?"

"Yeah, he came in. And no girl."

"So he went up to his room. That's excellent. What's his room number?"

"Fuck you."

"I need to talk to this guy," I said. "I'm a good person. I'm looking for this young girl for her family. I'm not going to make any trouble."

"Fuck you."

I took out another twenty and slid it through.

"Sixty-three," he said.

I waited nearly five minutes for the elevator and thought of walking up the stairs, but then kept on waiting. Finally, it came. I went up to the sixth floor, another long ride. I knocked at sixty-three and got no response. I could hear the TV playing inside, and playing in the other rooms on the hall. I knocked again, but with more force. I said, through the door, "I have a note for you from G." I thought that might rouse him. I waited. I put my ear against the door and didn't hear any movement. I tried the knob. Vincent Ettin was not big on locking doors. I let myself in. He was lying on the big queen-size bed, his arms splayed out. There was a band of rubber wrapped around Vincent's right arm and there was a needle still in his left hand.

I had never seen a dead body in my forty-two years and Vincent Ettin was my first.

Near a deli on Seventh Avenue and Twenty-eighth was a pay phone. It didn't work. I walked a few blocks south and found one that did work. It had been years since I used a pay phone. I called 911 and reported a dead body in the Senton Hotel on Twenty-eighth Street, room sixty-three. The operator wanted my name and I hung up. I called 911 again, spoke to a different operator, and told that person the same thing and hung up. I wanted to make sure they got it right.

Fifteen minutes before those phone calls, I had been in his room, just staring at the body, terrified and disbelieving, but then I'd had the presence of mind to close the door and I got on the bed right next to him. I cursed myself for not knowing CPR. *Do I pinch his nostrils and blow into his mouth? Do I pound on his chest?* His eyes were open, but they were like the eyes of a doll. I felt his neck for a pulse, feeling the skin beneath the tattoo, which was some obscure Asian markings, and there wasn't anything there, no pulse, no life. Then I put my head against his chest and I couldn't hear anything. But I opened his lips, anyway, and held his nose shut—it's what I had seen on TV—and I suppressed a scream of terror and blew air into him. I thought I might be sick. I did it for maybe twenty seconds and it had no effect. I pulled away. My first animal instinct had been correct—he was dead.

I staggered out of the room, sort of trembly and dizzy, but I walked down the six flights of stairs to get my head straight, and then went right out of the hotel, not handing in my key, not saying anything to my Indian pal. Just got out of there. Let him try to find Philip Marlowe.

After making the 911 calls and walking about twenty blocks in some kind of frenzied panic, spitting repeatedly to get the taste of the dead man out of my mouth, I hailed a cab to take me back to Brooklyn. In the car, I tried calling Lisa Weiss, hoping to end this nightmare and find the damn girl, but got the same fucking filled-up voice mail. I then tried calling Rachel Weiss, but she didn't pick up and I left a message, saying she should call me right away, though I tried to keep my voice calm. When I spoke to her, I was going to tell her to have her parents call the police right away. But I have to say, this scared me. What kind of trouble could I get into for taking on this whole thing and then anonymously reporting a dead body? But it didn't matter, I just had to get out of this mess.

I got home around twelve thirty and lay on top of my bed for hours, didn't even take off my sport coat or shoes, just lay there, numb, waiting for Rachel to call, but she never did. At some point, I passed out. I woke up around eight a.m. and called Rachel again and left another voice mail. At nine I tried her again and I got a recording telling me that the service at the number had been suspended. Fucking college student hadn't paid her bill and I needed to talk to her!

I thought of calling her parents but I didn't know where in Maryland they lived. I started pacing in my dirty apartment. I went on craigslist and called one of the private detectives listed. I told him most of my story, kept it real tight, except I didn't say anything about my bogus ad, just that I was a friend trying to help out.

"Why did you make an anonymous call to the cops?" the PI asked. He had a gruff voice.

"I don't know. I was scared."

"That doesn't look good. Makes it seem like you did something wrong. You and your friend better go to the police. It sounds like you stepped in a big pile of shit."

"Could you help us?" I asked. I hadn't told him about Vincent's dog, so he didn't know how accurate his metaphor was.

He was silent a moment, then he said, "I'm busy," and he hung up. He must not have liked the sound of the whole thing. I didn't blame him.

I tried Rachel's number again and got the same recording. I called Temple University information and the number they had for her was her cell phone.

Stay cool, I told myself. *Stay cool.* I undressed and took a shower.

I dried off and got dressed in the same clothes I had been wearing, except for the tie. Putting on fresh clothes seemed like too much to ask of myself. I tried Rachel and her sister just to torture myself, got the usual results, and I even thought for a moment of calling Vincent's number, and then I remembered that he was dead. I was already unraveled and it was getting worse.

I sat at my desk, staring at the computer, and I thought of calling the cops or going to the cops, my local precinct, but what would I say? I had posted a bogus ad, then given a false name to some undergrad from Temple University, run around the city, found a dead body, and made two anonymous calls to 911.

I filled my kettle to boil some water to make coffee in my French press. Marlowe was always making himself coffee. The thing to do was to stay calm and not overreact, that's how Marlowe always handled himself. While the water did its thing, I started dialing 911 again, to get this over with, but then I couldn't go through with it. I was too scared. I hung up the phone.

I poured myself a cup of coffee and sat back down at my desk, like it was any other day, and because I'm a sick person, I logged on to the backgammon site, thinking that a game might clear my head, and on the site the day was listed: April 20, 2007. I didn't start playing. I remembered the card from G. I took it out of my wallet. I held it, and sipped my coffee.

There were two competing thoughts in my head: (1) go to the cops right now, and (2) call G. Calling G had the appeal of a first drink on a relapse. You know you're going horribly against the grain, doing the wrong thing, what they call in the AA *Big Book* "a sickening rebellion," but there's some kind of mad force of nature that makes you do it, that demands that you do it. So before I could stop myself, in the grips of it, the impulse to self-destruct, to get deeper into this mess, I dialed *67 to block my number and then dialed the number on the card.

"Yeah." It was a deep voice. I was going off the deep end, but for once at least I didn't get somebody's fucking voice mail and that was a relief.

"Is this G?" I asked.

"Who's this?" There was some trace of a Spanish accent, but not much. "How'd you get my number?"

"I . . . I went to Lakes Bar, the bartender gave me your card. I've been looking for the girlfriend of Vincent Ettin. Lisa Weiss. Do you, by any chance, know where she is?"

"Where's Vincent at? Who is this?"

"Do you think you can help me?"

"What the fuck are you talking about? Help you with what?" The voice was angry, hostile, fierce.

"Finding this girl."

"Where's Vincent. I need to speak to him."

"This is going to sound strange. I don't know if you're good friends. But he's dead."

"What the fuck you saying?"

"I was looking for this girl, Lisa Weiss, and I found Vincent. He was in a hotel and he OD'd."

"This is fucked-up. You're a friend of Vincent's? Where are you?"

"I'm not a friend. I'm looking for the girl."

"How do you know he's dead if you're not a friend."

"I found him dead."

"You're fucking lying to me. Who are you? Tell me your fucking name."

"Jonathan Spencer. Do you know where the girl is?"

"Okay," he said, less heated. He was suddenly all calm and gentle. "I know Lisa. She's a friend. She's a good girl. You and I should meet up and talk this out. Figure out what is going on. Where do you live?"

"I'm in Brooklyn, but I'll meet you somewhere. Where are you?"

"I'm in Brooklyn. Red Hook. Come to where I work. You know Coffey Street, off of Van Brunt? You know Red Hook?"

"Yeah, it's not far from me. Where do you work?"

"C and L."

"What's C and L?"

"Beverage distributor."

"Okay . . . How about we meet at this restaurant in Red Hook—Hope and Anchor, you know that place? It's open for breakfast."

"Yeah, sure, I know it. We deliver to them."

"Want to meet there in half an hour?"

"Okay."

"And you'll tell me where Lisa is?"

"Yeah. Yeah."

"Can you just tell me on the phone, then?"

"Listen you f—" He reigned himself in. "I want to talk to you about Vincent, this shit about OD'ing. It's not something to talk about on the phone, hearing that someone you know is dead, if he is dead. So let's meet up and talk this shit out."

"All right, see you at the restaurant in half an hour. I'll be wearing a tan cap and a gray sport coat."

"I'll find you," he said, and hung up.

Like somebody sleepwalking and going out a ten-story window, not knowing what they're doing, I called Promenade car service, the one I always use. They came in fifteen minutes and ten minutes after that I was at Hope and Anchor, which I had been to a few times. It was almost ten thirty in the morning. It was a faux rustic little place—a cutesy, gentrified outpost in the old waterfront neighborhood of Red Hook, which in the last five years had started attracting artists, the kinds of people who fifteen years before had been colonizing the Williamsburg neighborhood of Brooklyn, and they colonized it so well that they can't afford to live there anymore. So now it's Red Hook.

The place was empty at ten thirty in the morning on a Friday, except for a scruffy twentysomething fellow drinking coffee and reading the *New York Times*, and the waitress, a cute hippie-looking blonde, also in her twenties. I ordered a coffee. I wasn't thinking about much. I was sort of high or something. High on the folly of all that I had been doing. But not high in a good way, more like I was out of it, dazed. It didn't help that I had probably slept only about three hours.

Then G came in. He was my height, about six feet, and had a muscular V-shaped torso discernible underneath a gray sweatshirt with a hood. He had shiny black hair, which was greased back, and he was good-looking, nice features—a straight, elegant nose, big eyes, masculine chin. He had light brown skin, and, like Shiny the bartender said, was probably in his early thirties. There was a scar on his right cheek, not too pronounced but visible. We made eye contact and I didn't like the way he looked at me. My heart stopped and he came over to me, sat right next to me, instead of across from me, put a switchblade right against my belly, and said, "Let's talk outside. I'll rip you up. I don't give a shit. Just walk out with me."

"I haven't paid for my coffee," I said. Why this occurred to me, I don't know.

"Put the money on the table and fucking walk out," he said. The waitress was sitting at the bar with her back to me, and the boy with his paper didn't even look up. Music was playing loudly on the stereo system. They were in their own worlds.

I put a five on the table, it was the smallest bill I had, and G walked behind me and led me outside to a big car, a sky blue Chevy Caprice, with fancy rims. I knew it was a Caprice. I'd had one years ago. He had a friend in the front seat at the wheel and we sat in the back.

We drove a few blocks and then turned right on Coffey, which is a long block of warehouses that leads to the waterfront and the moribund, long-dead Red Hook piers. Manhattan was across the river and to the right, gleaming and rich. Straight ahead, about half a mile away, was the Statue of Liberty. It was a beautiful day out—clear and bright.

Spanish music played on the radio and they didn't say anything. I hadn't gotten too good a look at the driver, but he seemed younger than G, probably in his early twenties, and from the back-seat I looked at his shiny black hair, which was cut close to his scalp, so you could see the skin between each individual hair. His neck and shoulders were fat. He was a fat boy.

"Is G your full name or just an initial?" I asked.

"Shut up," he said, and then said something in Spanish to the driver.

"Where's Lisa?" I said, pretending to be brave, and I sort of fooled myself in that I actually felt sort of brave.

"I told you to shut up."

We pulled into a garagelike warehouse, not too big, but room enough for the car and a van that was already parked and which had C & L BEVERAGES stenciled on its side. Toward the back of the garage there were dozens of piled-up cases of soda and water and beer.

We got out of the car. G pushed me toward the far-left corner, where there was a battered steel door. He stayed behind me, and I didn't feel the knife, but I knew it wasn't far away. His fat friend followed after us. We went through the door and into a crowded office that had more cases of water and soda stacked along its walls. On a little couch was Lisa Weiss, with thick gray tape over her mouth, and her wrists and ankles were also bound by tape. She was wearing a short black skirt and a white blouse, which was dirty and ripped by the right shoulder, like she had been yanked, and because of the tape around her ankles her knees were close together and prim-looking. The hollows of her eyes were darkened from exhaustion and smeared mascara, and she stared at me.

There was a battered desk next to the couch, and behind it was a squat, older man with gray in his short, close-cropped hair. He had a black moustache, also with traces of gray, and like G and the fat boy, he was Hispanic, with yellow-brown skin. He appeared to be in his midfifties and was wearing a blue short-sleeved sport shirt, with only two buttons and an open collar. He was smoking a cigarette and had a thin-lipped ugly mouth underneath his moustache. G pushed me forward so that I was standing right by the edge of the desk. The older man spoke to me.

"Where's Vincent?"

"I told G here that I found him dead last night of an overdose. At the Senton Hotel." The girl kicked out her legs, but nobody paid attention to her.

"Don't fucking lie to me," said the old man.

"I'm not, I swear . . . He had just shot up. He OD'd. I'm just looking for this girl." I pointed to Lisa. She kicked her legs again. "Her sister asked me to find her and I tracked down Vincent and found him dead."

"Are you fucking with me?" the old man asked, and G stuck me in the back with the knife, just enough so that I could feel the point coming through my sport coat.

"I'm not. I promise. I just want to take this girl and leave. I don't know what's going on."

"Your friend Vincent owes me seventy-five thousand dollars, one key. I told him he had to have it to me by *today*."

"He's not my friend."

"I gave him all the bars on Avenue B for dealing and he fucked me over. You can never trust a junkie. I have to say that it's my own damn fault." He seemed to be speaking more to G and the fat boy than to me.

"I don't know what's going on," I said. "But he's dead. I'm telling you the truth. You could call the Senton Hotel and ask them if someone died there last night. He was in room sixty-three."

The old man was quiet. "If he died, it wasn't our shit," he then said, not really to anyone.

He opened a drawer in his desk and then came around to my side. He was shorter and more squat than I realized, maybe five foot five, but there was a large black gun in his hand and so it didn't really matter. He said something to G in Spanish and G shoved me down to my knees. I don't think the old man liked me towering over him.

Then he pushed the gun against my mouth. "Open up," he said. I didn't. I glanced for a second at the girl; her eyes were terrified and she was kicking out her legs. G took a step toward her and she stopped the kicking. The old man said it again, "Open up," but I didn't. Then he smacked me across the jaw with the handle of the gun, making sure to hit the bone. I opened my mouth then and he put the gun inside. I tasted the grease and the metal.

"That bastard has nine lives. All junkies do. I don't think he's dead. He got away from these two *maricons*, jumping out a window, should have broken his neck then, and they bring me this Jewish bitch. I don't need her and I don't need you. I need Vincent. I want my money." He swirled the gun around in my mouth, knocking it gently against my teeth. I stared at his yellow hand holding the gun, his thick blunt fingers. Lisa must have been with Vincent at the apartment when G and the fat boy showed up; Vincent went out the window, left his cell phone, and they took the girl. I thought of that dog. "But he doesn't have my money," the old man went on, "and tells you to call G and act like he's dead to get out of it. So you fucking tell me where Vincent is hiding!"

"He's dead. OD'd," I said, and with the gun in my mouth I sounded horrific, like a deaf-mute, my words all strangled.

He violently raked the gun sideways out of my mouth, breaking my front teeth on purpose. I screamed and my mouth filled with blood.

Then he hit me across the face with the gun, doing it very hard this time, using the barrel like a knife and opening up my cheek.

"Is he really dead? Don't lie to me!"

"Yes. Please. Please. I'm sorry." I was begging and my mouth was bleeding, and my teeth were sharp, broken things. I put my hand to my face, to try to keep my cheek in one piece, I could feel it flapping open; I might have been going into shock, it was like I wasn't really there. I was detached and drifting away, passive and submissive. I had always wondered how so many Jews could be killed in Germany, but now I knew why they would get on their knees and be shot into their own open graves.

Then there was a spark of life in my mind, what I thought was a solution, and I said, "I went to his apartment. There was a lot of musical equipment in his bedroom. You could sell it and probably make some of your money back. I'll help you, I promise. That's probably where a lot of the money went."

My words were all mangled and came out sibilant because of my teeth, and the old man looked at me like I was crazy. Then he handed the gun to G and muttered something in Spanish, and I couldn't have possibly seen it, but I felt like I did, some kind of Darwin thing where an animal, a human animal like me, can see things it shouldn't. So I saw G swinging the gun down at the back of my head and then my head and eyes were filled with a red-orange color and there was a burning pain at the base of my neck, my spine itself was in an agony it had never felt before, and then there was blackness, like a sudden, violent suffocation.

When I came to I thought I was in a dark metal box, I couldn't really see anything, and there was something soft next to my face. I reached across myself and ran my hand over the soft thing and my eyes adjusted to the minimal light and I saw that I was touching Lisa Weiss's leg. She was still taped up and she had passed out. We were moving, and I realized I was lying in the back of what must have been the van I had seen in the garage. There were a few cases of Poland Spring water and there were two frosted-over windows on the back doors and they let in just enough milky light for me to make things out. It was a closed-off compartment, and whoever was driving the van was on the other side of the aluminum-sheet wall behind me. I touched my face. It was dried and swollen, but there was a long hole, a groove I could put my finger in. I felt horrified and I sat up. I ran my tongue over my jagged teeth and I looked at my watch. It was almost nine p.m.; I had been out for hours. I reached behind my head and felt a swelling back there that was the size of a tennis ball. I shook Lisa but she didn't wake up.

I felt for my cell phone and wallet, but they were both gone. I slid down to the doors, but there were no inside handles. I tried to look out the windows, but I couldn't see anything. I was incredibly thirsty and it seemed like odd luck that there were cases of water. I pulled a bottle out of one of the boxes and I took a sip but I could barely swallow.

We were driving somewhere very bumpy and I spilled most of the water on myself, but what little I was able to get down tasted good. I looked again at my watch. I couldn't believe how long I had been out. I figured they had waited until it was dark so that they would have the cover of night for killing us and getting rid of our bodies.

They must have followed up, after all, on what I told them about Vincent, and without him the girl was just a liability, no longer a bargaining chip, just somebody they had kidnapped, so better to get rid of her; and me, well, I was a fool that they had absolutely no use for and if I was dead, then I couldn't make trouble for them. They had a good setup: they distributed beverages and heroin, and that's probably how they met Vincent. The beverages got them in the door at bars and then they hooked up bartenders to deal for them. They dealt in two substances that people needed, and the liquids probably cleaned the cash from the drugs.

I looked around me. I didn't want to die. I had to do something to help me and this girl. In the murky shadows I made out a spare tire attached to the wall of the van. I thought maybe I could use the tire to bang open the door. It was a futile thought, but I tried to take the tire off the wall and I saw that inside it was a jack and a tire iron. I yanked out the iron. One end was shaped like an egg holder for unscrewing lug nuts, and the other end was a sharpish wedge for prying off hubcaps. The van came to a stop. I got to my feet. I could just about stand near the two doors, bending over a little. My head was pounding. I held the tire iron like a club, the lug nut end in my fist.

The doors opened up and it was the fat boy and I came down on his face with the tire iron as hard as I could and the thing went right through his nose and deep into his face and got stuck there. I fell forward and he fell back onto the ground and I landed on top of him and it was a freakish thing but that tire iron, with my weight behind it, pierced deeper into his flesh and must have gone right into his brain.

A car door slammed toward the front of the van and I scrambled around and saw that the fat boy had a gun tucked into his pants. I yanked that out, sprawling across him, my stomach on his thick legs, and G came around, talking on his cell phone, probably to a girl; he was saying, "Okay, baby," and he was five feet from me and he said, "Oh, fuck," and I had the gun pointed right at him. I pulled the trigger and nothing happened. It was on safety.

G dropped his phone and reached for his own gun, which was in a large pocket in the side of his pants, and I flipped the safety—my dad had guns when I was a kid and I knew where the safety was— and I shot at G and somehow I missed and he was bent over, struggling with the Velcro on his pocket, and I fired again and it went right through the top of his sleek black head and he went down.

I looked around me. We were near the water, the edge of the Atlantic Ocean. I could see the Verrazano Bridge to the north. We were on some bumpy, broken-up service road off the Belt Parkway. High weeds and concrete barriers hid us from view, but high-powered streetlights from the highway, about two hundred yards away, cast everything in silvery shadows and light came off the water like a mirror.

G and the fat boy were probably going to shoot us and then dump us in the current. I dropped the gun and went into the van. I shook Lisa and poured a bottle of water on her face and she still wouldn't wake up. I worried about hurting her, but I yanked off her mouth tape and vomit spilled out. I realized she was dead. She must have vomited behind that tape and choked to death.

Somehow, shifting their bodies a little at a time, I got G and his friend into the back of the van and closed them in there with Lisa. I looked for my phone on G and the fat boy, but they didn't have it, and they also didn't have my wallet. So I thought of using G's phone to call the police, but then I felt like I had to keep moving; I didn't want to wait for the cops to come to me. I started the van up, found my way out to the highway, and decided to go to my own neighborhood, to go to *my* precinct. It was some kind of muted desire to just go home, but I knew I couldn't go home just yet, so the best I could do was go to the police *near my home*.

And I knew I had to go to them. I had killed two men and I had more or less killed this girl I had never really met. If I hadn't interfered, they might have let her go. Without me bringing the news, it could have been awhile before they found out Vincent was dead, if they ever did find out, and so they probably would have just threatened her, said they'd be watching her until Vincent showed up. She'd still have value to them as a link to their money and so she'd be alive, and maybe she would have been smart and gotten far away from New York. She could have been safe. But I had complicated everything and so because of me she was dead.

I drove north on the Belt, and the lights of the oncoming traffic were killing my eyes. I knew I must have a bad concussion and I couldn't stop morbidly running my tongue over my fractured teeth, which made me think of the old man in the garage. I didn't like the fact that he probably had my phone and my wallet. Maybe I wouldn't be able to pin anything on him and he'd come after me. He could find me.

So I changed my mind and I didn't go immediately to the police. I drove over to Coffey Street and pulled into the garage. The blue Caprice was there and there was a light under the door in the corner. I don't think he was expecting me and I had the fat boy's gun in my hand.

McSweeney's Issue 24, 2007

JOURNALISM

An Open Diary

I sit on the 7 train, heading to the U.S. Open, and I admire the shapely calves of the woman sitting next to me. She's talking to two colleagues who stand in front of her, and they're all going to the Open. One of her colleagues is a fey young man, who bears an uncanny resemblance, especially considering our destination, to Pete Sampras. The other colleague, a middle-aged woman, appears to be the boss, and she's gossiping about someone in their office: "She's gone on four dates with this guy who is categorically handsome, but he hasn't made a move. He's not aggressive enough."

"Four dates?" says the woman next to me.

"That's a lot of dates," says Pete Sampras.

"She's the third woman I know who said she's dating someone who's not aggressive," says the boss.

I wonder what's going on with these passive men, some of whom are categorically handsome, and then I tune the trio out. I tell myself I should be thinking about tennis, after all I'm on assignment. For some reason my mind then flashes back to this town tennis tournament I won the summer before eighth grade. I was supposed to get a trophy, but it wasn't ready when I won. The guy in charge of the tournament and the trophies was this fellow who had a withered leg from polio. He was in his late forties and the town paid him a small fee to be in charge of all things tennis. He loved the sport and was constantly playing, heroically dragging that leg all over the court.

I had two baseball trophies, two soccer trophies, and one fake, unearned trophy, which featured an athlete in a bathing suit, and I desperately wanted to replace the false trophy with my tennis trophy. Five trophies would really show the world what an athlete I was. How the world would know this I'm not sure, since no one ever came into my room other than my mother.

So I started calling the man with the bad leg every two weeks, asking him if my trophy had arrived yet. After about four months of phone calls, he yelled: "It's just a trophy. Stop calling me!" Then one day, about six months after I won the tournament, he put the trophy in our mailbox. I positioned it on my bureau where I could stare at it narcissistically for hours, but it was a bit tainted now since I had tormented the tennis guy to get it. I was the town champ but I still felt like a loser—my life story.

4:00 P.M.

I'm outside the press office at the tennis center, waiting for my credentials, and I spot Virginia Wade, the former British champion. She's tan, handsome, and dignified, with gray hair feathered down the middle. Then I spot the beautiful Maria Sharapova coming from the practice courts. She's in a halter top and sweatpants, and I can see that beneath the sweatpants, though she is thin and tall, she has powerful buttocks, which must aid her serve. Sharapova then disappears into the players' entrance to the stadium, and I admire, on my right, a policeman with a German shepherd. The dog is panting from the heat and lying down on the job. I see that on the back of the policeman's shirt it says *Canine Unit*. Ever since I was a child I've wanted to be a policeman and I'm also madly in love with dogs, so I write in my little notebook that being a part of the Canine Unit would be the best of both worlds for me, and then I remember how years ago a transsexual prostitute in the Meatpacking District whispered to me, like a siren, as I walked by, "It's the best of both worlds," and then a girl in the press office comes outside and tells me that my credentials are ready.

7:30 P.M.

I'm sitting in the journalists' section of Arthur Ashe stadium. The humidity is as thick as a phone book. It's like being in a bathroom with the windows closed after taking an epically long, hot shower. I'm wearing a linen blazer which feels as comfortable as a suture. To my right, about fifty yards away, Mayor Bloomberg and former mayor Dinkins, both in suit and tie, seem impervious to the heat.

Maria Sharapova is playing a Greek woman named Daniilidou. Sharapova is in a light blue dress with yellow trim and no sleeves. The dress flaps up when she exerts herself and you see bright yellow undergarments, which aren't really panties but the kind of thing that a superheroine might wear—a cross between panties and tights.

When she serves, I note that her armpits are quite white, as opposed to her tan outer arms, and I find this very sexy. I've always had a thing for women's armpits. It's not an all-consuming thing, like a foot fetish, but just a general admiration for the female armpit.

Sitting near Mayor Bloomberg, Andy Rooney is hunched over in a posture that would seem to indicate rapt attention, but on closer inspection, I can see that his spine has been crushed by age and time, though it doesn't mean he's not paying attention. David Boies, Al Gore's lawyer, sits a few rows behind Rooney, and my mind drifts back to the 2000 election, but it doesn't like to drift back there for too long.

From the upper reaches of the stadium a man cries out, "I love you, Maria!"

She wins in straight sets.

9:30 P.M.

Andre Agassi is playing superbly and is easily defeating his opponent, a guy named Razvan Sabau. Women call out, "I love you, Andre!"

Agassi seems to waddle a little and I imagine that his body, after running thousands of miles on tennis courts all over the world, is a bit worn down, but he still hits the ball with great authority.

I wonder what keeps Agassi going—this is his twentieth year playing the U.S. Open. Isn't he bored with it? Then I think how being competitive never goes away. It's instinctual, like lust. No matter how much you've made love you're still, more or less, interested in sex. I, for example, never play competitive sports anymore, but I do play Internet backgammon against anonymous strangers and I find myself wanting to win. But why? Who cares? It must be Darwinian. To prove you are the best is part of our programming, because if you're the best, then you get to have a mate and you get to pass on your genes. Why we want to pass on our genes, I don't know, but seemingly we do. So this desire to pass on one's genes fools one into striving, even at Internet backgammon or professional tennis. Something like that. Well, we've all been hearing about intelligent design and I've just now given an example of ignorant Darwinism.

10:45 P.M.

I'm in the interview room with many journalists. Agassi, who has won his match quickly and efficiently, comes in. He has white threads hanging from his chin, which he is unaware of. He must have dried his face with a towel that was falling apart.

He fields a number of dull questions with patience and generosity. I then work up the courage and ask, "Do you ever feel bad defeating your opponents? You handily beat that guy tonight and it was his first U.S. Open."

Agassi looks me right in the eye and says, firmly, "No. You don't cheat anybody out of their experience. It all makes you who you are down the road. You've got to learn from it. I've been on the other side."

I love his answer. It's the thinking of a champion, but it's also quasi-spiritual, acknowledging the other player's destiny. Then I think how I let my best friend, when I was fourteen, beat me at tennis. I had been defeating him for years, and so this one time I finally let him win and when we were done he lorded his victory over me. He carried on for several minutes and then I weakened and said, "You only won because I let you." This resulted in a terrible fight and we never played tennis again.

SEPTEMBER 2, 2005
4:00 P.M.

Serena Williams is playing an Italian woman named Francesca Schiavone. Serena has very appealing, well-defined armpits, and her superheroine panties are burgundy. When she walks, her rear seems to have a life of its own, and a very nice life at that.

It's a bright, beautiful day, and above us the Fuji blimp makes a loud, droning sound, like an enormous, noisy refrigerator in the sky, and men call out, "I love you, Serena!"

I'm sitting with a bunch of salty old journalists. Bud Collins, the legendary jovial tennis maven, is directly in front of me and I say to him, "Excuse me, Mr. Collins, but I was wondering, do you know when fans started shouting out 'I love you' to the players?"

"I first heard it a century ago," says Collins, "in Boston. Someone shouted 'I love you, Cooz!' to Bob Cousy. I'm not sure when it started in tennis. They get some sort of self-fulfillment proclaiming it."

Then Collins says to a man to our left, "Would you please sit down, sir," and I see that it's Richard Williams, Serena's father. He turns and smiles at Collins, who was, of course, joking, and says, "If I sit down I won't be able to get up."

Serena is playing inconsistently but winning. She's too much for Schiavone. During tough points, her father, with a slight lisp, encourages, "Come on, Serena!"

An old Italian journalist next to me says to an even older American journalist, "You know what Schiavone means?"

"No," says the old, weather-beaten American. These guys are a fraternity of tennis-press and they enjoy teasing each other.

"Big slave," says the Italian.

Bud Collins turns around and says, "It means big slave?"

"Yes," says the well-spoken Italian. "I have to talk to you, Bud, about these things, not this old alligator"—referring to the weathered American journo—"who can't understand nuance. He's not civilized."

"Go, big slave," says the old American.

5:10 P.M.

I'm in the corridor of the stadium. Serena has won. Two journalists are speaking with Richard Williams. I approach and they peel away and I say to Mr. Williams, in journalist mode, "You hear so much about the American dream, but I think you're an authentic dreamer. You envisioned your two daughters as champions and it came true."

"I wanted them to be number one and number two in the world, but I was a fool then," he says.

"What would be your goal now?" I ask, surprised by what he has said.

"Unity of the family," he says, a bit forlornly, and then we part, and I don't know the full story, but I think he must be broken-hearted that his marriage has failed.

6:00 P.M.

I'm in the interview room and Serena Williams is fielding questions. She's eloquent and charming. I ask her: "Amidst all the calls of 'Come on, Serena!' are you able to make out your father's voice?"

"I can kind of differentiate my dad's voice," she says. "I definitely listen for it innately."

"Does it help you when you hear him?"

"I think it does," she says sweetly. "I think it does."

I'm tempted to ask her about her father's statement about family unity, but it doesn't seem necessary.

9:50 P.M.

The air temperature is pleasant. It's the kind of night that makes you forget about global warming for half an hour, and Roger Federer, the number one man, is playing a wily Frenchman named Santoro. Federer walks about the court with great self-possession, seemingly unflappable. His eyes are set a bit too close together, otherwise he'd be matinee-idol handsome.

In the VIP section, Nicole Kidman, ethereal with her yellow-blonde hair and luminous skin, leans back in her chair, calmly elegant, like a twenty-first-century Grace Kelly. She sits with the director Steven Shainberg, who has cast her as Diane Arbus in his latest film. I watch her watch Federer. It all feels vaguely Roman—he's a gladiator and she's an empress—except no one's life is at stake, only money, and lots of it. I wonder if she finds Federer appealing. I imagine myself talking to her, how I would fumble for words, like a fool.

11:00 P.M.

I lie on a bench near the enormous World's Fair globe, which is just outside the tennis center. Fountains go about their business of shooting water in the air. I look up into the black night sky. I'm a bit lonely and I think about my failings as a person. Then I give it a rest and just look into the sky and for a moment I feel at peace on a beautiful summer night.

The New York Observer, 2005

Middle-American Gothic

I'm forty-one years old and outwardly I may be one of the least Goth people you could ever meet. For more than a decade, my style, fashion-wise, has been faux-preppy English professor, which means I wear sport coats and corduroy pants. To add a touch of flair, and to hide my bald head, I wear a tan cap backward, such that it looks like a beret. My musical taste, I should tell you, is similar to my clothing, which is to say it is decidedly non-Goth. Twenty years ago, in college, I listened primarily to Cat Stevens, James Taylor, and Simon & Garfunkel; recently I've discovered Radiohead and find them to be quite good. So, clearly, I'm some kind of musical idiot.

Thus, *Spin*, being rather mischievous, thought I'd be the perfect person to cover Gothicfest 2005, which was the first of its kind, just as there once was a first Super Bowl or World War. It was an all-day gathering of twenty Goth bands in Villa Park, Illinois, a distant suburb of Chicago. The following is a diary of my adventures amid these dark minstrels and their loyal fans.

SATURDAY, SEPTEMBER 17, 2005
THE ODEUM SPORTS & EXPO CENTER
12:25 P.M.

I'm wearing my checked sport coat, white shirt, tan cap, and jeans (to help me fit in a little), but I already seem to be attracting stares.

There are roughly one hundred people mingling about, and the Halloweenish costumes are causing a knee-jerk terror response in me. There's also pounding, scary music being played by a DJ. I may have subconsciously chosen a white shirt to be defiant—everyone else is, of course, in black—and I just fantasized about being beaten to death as an intruder, getting kicked repeatedly while lying on the ground. A few of the fellows here look like neo-Nazi skinheads, which, I think, provoked this beating-to-death fantasy; also, I'm a little depressed and that always brings on suicidal thoughts.

Two chubby, expressionless boys stand to my right. They were once cute children, but now I imagine that they spend hours in dark bedrooms looking at violent porn. Or perhaps they have tender reveries about being sweet to the girls who they adore from a distance. I'd like to think about them in this generous light—that they are actually gentle young men—but it's hard not to stereotype them as potential serial killers. It's their eerie, still blankness that makes me think they're capable of murder—and the fact that I'm in the Midwest. The Midwest seems to cultivate serial killing. Must be the boxed-in geography.

One wears glasses and has multipierced ears and a scruffy pubescent beard. His hair is dyed red and spiked up. His dirty, loose jeans flow to the floor over his shoes. His friend has a more mature beard but is fatter and shorter, and his nose is swollen with oil and clogged pores. His eyes are slits. He wears a winter hat, a dirty T-shirt, and filthy jeans. He really could be a medieval Visigoth; I can imagine him swinging an ax with vigor. I do like that these two are standing next to each other, that they are friends and are here together. It makes me think of my childhood best friend, whom I hadn't seen for years, and then I learned two years ago that he had died. I miss him. In fact, I dreamed about him last night. Every few months I dream that we're friends again.

12:45 P.M.

The Odeum Sports & Expo Center resembles an airplane hangar, with bleachers on one side. There are no windows, and though it's midday, it feels like night, which is fitting. There's a concession area at one end and a very large stage at the other. There are also about two dozen booths, selling various Goth goods: CDs, black capes, plastic skulls, human skeletons, knives, and Vampire Wine. It's just wine, but when you drink it, I guess you pretend that it's blood. It reminds me of how, when I was a kid, you could get chocolate cigars and cigarettes and pretend you were an adult.

The first band, Dead Girls Corp., has just started playing. The singer keeps reminding the audience that they have driven all the way from California. He wants us to appreciate this sacrifice, which is understandable, but mentioning it repeatedly is a little tiresome. "Feeling empty because there's something to say," he sings. Shouldn't it be, "because there's nothing to say"? Then again, he might be right. All we really can express is pain. This diary and everything else I've ever written is actually a code for one word: help!

A fellow to my right is wearing a T-shirt that promotes the film *American Psycho*. Another young man's shirt says *Biohazard Level 4*. It occurs to me that I'm inwardly apocalyptic and these people are outwardly apocalyptic. I may dress like a somewhat libidinous college professor, but in my heart of hearts, I'm in a state of dark despair about the world. But are these people embracing the apocalypse, while I'm nervously awaiting it? I may not look the part, but in my own way, I belong here.

1:15 P.M.

I'm in a side room reserved for bands, talking to the ceremonial host and hostess of Gothicfest, Mark and Michelle.

Mark, nineteen, is wispy, with large, vulnerable eyes and dark hair draped across his forehead. He wears a black shirt, a velvet scarf, and saddle shoes. His black jeans are decorated with the lyrics from a song he wrote, "Crimson Tears of Tragedy."

Michelle, thirty-five, is short, pale, and voluptuous. She's got on a black satin ball gown made in Germany from a sixteenth-century design, bejeweled gloves, platform boots, and an elaborate dreadlocked hairpiece.

"What do you get out of the Goth scene?" I ask.

"The beauty of it," says Michelle. "The elegance. The history. There's so much conformity. We're nonconformists. We don't judge and we don't want to be judged. We're just artists expressing ourselves. I'm into traditional Goth: Bauhaus and Joy Division. I hold true to the people who started the movement. My look is more classic, elegant, but some days I can go cyber."

"I fall more into the glam-Goth scene," says Mark. "My idols were, like, David Bowie."

"I've sort of noticed that some people look like neo-Nazis," I say. "What do you guys think of that?"

"Some Goths use the Nazi symbol as a universal symbol of pain," says Michelle.

"Gothic culture," says Mark, "is torn. Some follow the Nazi beliefs or use swastikas as a sign of defiance."

"The Nazis would have taken people like this and killed them," I say.

"I know," says Mark.

"What do your families think about you being Goths?" I then ask.

"My mother loved the scene," says Michelle. "Like Peter Murphy. My father is totally sympathetic. Even when I was younger, into punk, he said, 'I will never have a square daughter.'"

"I live with my grandparents," Mark says. "My grandfather loves me for what I do—that I express myself. But my grandmother throws temper tantrums, calls me a fag because I wear makeup and I'm very feminine. I have an abusive relationship with my father. Constant beatings. I saw him in July, and he beat the shit out of me."

"Did you fight back?" I ask.

"I don't fight back," Mark says. "As much as I don't like him, I love him because he's my father. So I just take it. He wants me to be more of a man, not so fem. He wants me to be tougher, cold, heartless, an alpha male."

Later, Mark tells us how his uncle, a Goth who had drug problems but was a true father to him, committed suicide by slashing himself. Mark found him as he was bleeding to death. Mark starts crying and Michelle and I try to comfort him.

"I'm sorry I'm crying," he says.

"It's all right," I say.

2:20 P.M.

A band called Drake is playing. The lead singer wears a long robe. He chants into the microphone in an ominous, froggy voice: "Dost thou leave me with such a myth / Falling into the abyss." I admire his rhyme scheme, but it would be much better if he had a lisp—"the abyth."

I eyeball the young man next to me, who is thin, brown-haired, and not very Goth, except for his arms, which are encased in black fishnet stockings.

"Excuse me, could I interview you?" I ask.

"Sure," he says. "They call me Rain."

"Who's they?"

"The people at my college. I used to have purple hair and they weren't used to that there, so they called me Purple Rain, and it got shortened to Rain. My real name is Tim, but every Tim I know is a Melvin—an idiot—so I kept Rain."

"Are you still in college?"

"No, I'm thirty."

"What's your take on Gothicfest?" I ask.

"Well, I'm here for the headliner, Hanzel und Gretyl. I'm actually more into industrial. Most of the bands here today are industrial. Goth is dying. The scene is, like, twenty years old. It should die. It's all regurgitating what was done in Germany ten, twelve years ago. Goth now is more about the clothing than the music. You can buy Goth stuff at Hot Topic in the malls. Goth is dead in my world because it's packaged. It's not counterculture; it's pop culture . . . Have you read Chomsky?"

"Not really," I say, embarrassed, and then add weakly, "I have a sense, though, of what Chomsky is about."

"A lot of the political message of industrial is voicing what Chomsky says—that we live in a benevolent fascist state."

"I really need to read Chomsky," I say. "Immediately."

"You should see this documentary about him, *Manufacturing Consent*."

"Thanks for the tip," I say, and I sheepishly take my leave. I wasn't expecting to meet a Noam Chomsky fan at Gothicfest.

3:10 P.M.

A band with female members, Ghost Orgy, is onstage. They have a lovely, femme fatale–ish violinist and a busty lead singer in high black boots. There are about four hundred people here now, sporting a number of interesting T-shirt slogans: *Eat a bag of shit*; *Fuck you, you fucking fuck*; and *An experiment in sickness*. A girl walks past me with a backpack shaped like a coffin.

The singer suddenly lifts up her skirt, revealing black panties, and I think to myself that I very much need to interview this young lady.

3:40 P.M.

I'm sitting with Ghost Orgy's Dina Concina, who is in her mid-twenties and even more beautiful up close. I compliment her on her performance, discreetly not mentioning the lifting-of-the-skirt part. She says she started her music career as a rock 'n' roll singer but that she's been into Goth for the last three years.

"I realized how much hate I have inside," she says, explaining her transition. "And I get to channel it onstage."

"What do you hate?" I ask.

"Our corporate jobs, shit like that. People. Our lives."

"Why do you hate your life?"

"Because I work a corporate job. Well, I just quit. But I was an engineer scientist for Kraft Foods."

"What's an engineer scientist do?"

"I created the recipes for cookies and crackers. I launched the new Cheese Nips. They're fucking good. You should try them."

"What do your parents think about you being in a Goth band?"

"They don't even know the name of my band. They would kill me. They're old-school Filipino parents. But they're awesome. They know I'm in a band, but they don't know that I'm singing about death and demons and blood."

"They don't subscribe to *Spin*, do they?"

She smiles, and then tells me that her neck is very stiff—she wrenched it onstage. "I could give you a neck rub," I say, and I can't believe these words have come out of my mouth. It's like I have Tourette's. There's nothing more pathetic than a man who offers a beautiful young woman a massage.

"That would be great," she says. First a Chomsky fan and now a young woman who will let me touch her! This Gothicfest is rather remarkable.

I stand behind her and knead her neck. I feel like a dirty old man, and then I remember, I am a dirty old man.

4:10 P.M.

I'm in the bleachers with Steve Watson and his twelve-year-old daughter, Bethany, who are finishing up some hot dogs. Steve, fifty-three, is friendly and articulate. He's wearing khaki pants and a golf shirt. Bethany is frail and cute, with black lipstick, a retainer on her teeth, and a tiara on her dark hair.

"Bethany is into all kinds of music," Steve says. "Punk. Metal. And, quite frankly, I enjoy it as well. Living where we live, we're not exposed to all this." He waves his hand in front of him.

"You're a very open-minded parent," I say.

"I try to be. The community where we live is very affluent, and the people there are very intolerant. Not only are they intolerant of other people racially and financially, but if you don't fit in to the WASP lifestyle, you're shunned. Luckily for me, I have sufficient income so that I can say 'Fuck you.'"

"Why do you live there?"

"Economic advantages. Schools are very good. Crime is zero. But it's not a utopia. Everybody is forced into conformity, and it puts the kids under a lot of stress. Bethany had some friends who wanted to come today, but their parents wouldn't let them. I tell you, we're treated more openly and accepting at these concerts than in our own community."

Bethany tells me she had a band but that they split up. Their name was Toxic Popsicle. "Not your average prom queen," Steve tells me. "But I'm cool with it."

6:30 P.M.

A band called Reverend Agony is finishing up their set and the lead singer screams out: "Buy our album, *Staring into the Abyss*. I fucking love all of you and want to fuck all of you, so come up to me after the show!"

"Abyss" is clearly a popular word in the Goth scene, and I appreciate this fellow's ballsy honesty. There are about five hundred people here now, and many of them are cute Gothic girls wearing waist-cinchers which push their breasts up rather appealingly.

7:15 P.M.

I pass an empty booth, which only has a placard that reads *Satanic-sluts.com*. Title-wise this seems to be an intriguing website, perhaps worth visiting.

I keep walking and then I stop at the booth selling skulls. They are very realistic-looking and can be used as piggy banks and candleholders. The short, smiling proprietress says, "Everybody likes a little head."

"What did you say?" I ask. The music is very loud.

"Everybody likes a little head."

"What?"

"Everybody likes a little head."

I finally get what she's saying—she's making reference to her wares, the small skulls. I nod politely and her male coworker explains to me her sense of humor: "We usually work biker shows."

I move to the next stall, which is selling gigantic swords. I ask the woman standing behind a glass case of knives, "You can sell this stuff to someone right now?"

"No," she says. "At the end of the concert, they can get it, and then they're escorted out by security."

"That's good to know."

9:35 P.M.

I'm standing with two boys in the back of the center; they're both sixteen. Gerald is black and quite tall—about six-two. He's husky and has a sweet, open face. His only Gothish apparel is a long gray trench coat. His friend, Joey, is by comparison rather short—he's about five-six and wears a fishnet top and ripped jeans, and has a cherubic face, but his eyes, which are circled with black eyeliner, are wounded-looking. His hair is blond and spiky, and he has multiple earrings. Gerald is the only black person I've seen at Gothicfest.

"What brought you guys here today?" I ask.

"We're hoping to meet girls," says Gerald.

"Yeah," says Joey. "We're a good combo—they can get tall, dark, and handsome with him, or short and sexy with me."

"I don't mean to be rude," I say, addressing Gerald, "but I think you're the only black person here."

"Yeah, most black kids are into rap," he says, "but I like all kinds of music. I like industrial and Goth for the power. I like the whole scene." He puts his hand on his friend's shoulder. "We tried drinking our blood, but it wasn't our thing."

I learn that Joey has been in and out of about a dozen foster homes during the course of his life, and is probably moving again, and will most likely be separated from Gerald and put into a different school, which has both of them a little worried. They're best friends, having met two years ago.

"We watch each other's back," says Joey.

"We combine our powers," says Gerald. "He's got speed and I have strength."

I can see that they're a bit anxious to get closer to the dance floor, where the girls are, so I say, "Well, thanks for talking. I hope you meet some girls."

"Me, too," says Gerald, and we all shake hands and they walk off. Like with the two boys I had seen earlier, I'm touched by their friendship and I long, myself, to have a best friend. Someone to watch my back.

12:00 A.M.

I'm exhausted. I've been listening to Goth music for almost twelve hours. The last band is on, but I can't take much more. There are about seven hundred people here now—Gothicfest isn't a mad success, but it's not a failure, either. It's been a good day for the Goths. A pretty girl gyrating next to me shouts over the music, "Dance with me!"

"I'm too old," I say.

"No, you're not," she says.

"How old are you?" I ask. She looks about nineteen, twenty.

"Fifteen," she says.

"Have a good time," I say, and quickly head for the exit.

On my way out, I pass a fellow with spikes poking out of the top of his shaved head. It's like there are miniature traffic cones dividing his cranium in half.

"Are those spikes screwed into your skull?" I ask incredulously.

He puts his hand in his pocket, takes out a small bottle of glue, and says, "I'm not dumb, you know."

I nod and leave. Outside, there's a large, jaundiced moon in the black sky. I hope it's still there when the Goths come out. I feel like a parent whose children prefer to stay inside and watch TV. The father pleads, "It's a beautiful day. Why don't you go play outside?" In this case, I feel like pleading, "It's a completely spooky night. Forget the loud music, come outside and have a blood sacrifice or something! There's a full moon!"

But I don't say anything to anyone. I bid a silent farewell to the Expo Center, and with the moon watching over me, I get the hell out of there.

Spin, 2006

This essay was also selected for and published in The Best American Nonre-quired Reading 2007 *(Houghton Mifflin), edited by Dave Eggers.*

The Corduroy Appreciation Club

A few months ago, the executive director and founder of the Corduroy Appreciation Club, Miles Rohan, sent me an e-mail, requesting that I be the keynote speaker at his club's annual gathering on November 11. This date, Mr. Rohan informed me, was chosen because it is the date that "most resembles corduroy." I found the absurdity of the situation appealing and so I readily agreed. I didn't know why, though, I qualified as a keynote speaker for such a club, so in case there was some kind of misunderstanding, I did state in my acceptance e-mail that while a fan of corduroy, I was no aficionado of the fabric. I also inquired as to why I had been selected and Mr. Rohan wrote back that he was a fan of my writing. I found this, on an ego level, to be a sufficient explanation. I did wonder what I might say to rally the appreciators of corduroy, but as the meeting was in the future, I put the whole thing out of my mind.

But then November 11 was nearly upon me and Mr. Rohan wanted to meet me beforehand to go over a few things. Since we are both Brooklyn residents, we set a rendezvous at Gorilla Coffee on Fifth Avenue in Park Slope. The club meeting was also to be held in Park Slope, at the venerable Montauk Club on Eighth Avenue.

I sat on a bench outside Gorilla, reading a paper, and then suddenly standing before me was Mr. Rohan. He is a thirty-year-old man of decent height, about six foot, with a full head of curly brown hair. He was wearing corduroy pants (tan), jacket (darker tan), and tie (brown). His shirt was simple white cotton and his shoes were suede Wallabees. His eyes are a startling light green and he had a nervous but nearly mischievous smile, which is how I would characterize him in general—a bit nervous with a taste for mischief. Mischief of a certain, subtle kind, that is. Like starting a club with corduroy as its spiritual center.

We talked for quite some time on that bench. Naturally, I inquired how he came to create such a club, a club with 832 corduroy-loving members and with an international chapter opening in London. He explained to me that as a child he saw his older brother, by seven years, wearing corduroy, and he made an association with corduroy and "sophistication." He then wore some corduroy himself, but it "fell out of fashion in the eighties."

Then in 1999 Mr. Rohan was working in Bolivia at an English-language newspaper and in an orphanage. "It was in Bolivia that my interest in corduroy was reignited," he said. "When you drop clothing in Goodwill boxes, it ends up in places like Bolivia, being sold in stores, and there was so much corduroy and it was all so good, from the seventies, that I started buying it up, lots of it, and at first my friend Phil thought I was insane, he was also in Bolivia, but now he's opening the London chapter."

"What makes some corduroy 'good'?" I asked.

"Well, some corduroy has polyester and that's not as good," he said.

"How can you tell?" I asked. "Are my pants 'good'?" In honor of our meeting, I was wearing green corduroy pants.

"They look good," he said. "If there's polyester, I've been told, they make a funny smell if they catch on fire, but I don't think we should experiment on you."

"I agree," I said.

After returning from Bolivia in 2000, the idea of a corduroy club began to grow in Mr. Rohan's mind. "Initially, I just thought of having a corduroy party," he said, "but I also wanted to have a club, a social club. I like the idea of the Masons, the Elks, and secret societies, like Skull and Bones. My uncle, for example, is a Knight of Columbus. And I wondered why there weren't new clubs. And then I thought, why can't I have a club of my own?"

Mr. Rohan also intimated that at first he thought a corduroy club might be a good way to "meet girls." He did meet a girl, but not through his club, and now this girl was his wife of fourteen months, and Mr. Rohan told me that she was a bit worried about the money he was spending on the club—he worked as a digital archivist at Nickelodeon—and that his conversation was "limited to one topic." He also told me that she was very supportive and that she designed all the invitations, which were backed with corduroy, and the membership cards, which were also backed with corduroy.

I was glad to hear that his young marriage was not being completely torn apart by the club and then I asked, "And the point of a social club is to *socialize*?"

"I like to use the word 'fellowship,'" he said. "I went on a tour of the Masonic Temple on Twenty-third Street—for purposes of research—and I saw that they use the word 'fellowship' a lot and I liked that. It's all sort of silly, of course, but it's also serious. People are coming from all over for the meeting and they enjoy it."

The first meeting was held on November 11 (11/11), 2005, and the second meeting was held on January 11, 2006, since January 11 (1/11) is the date that, after November 11 (11/11), most nearly resembles corduroy.

Before we parted, I asked Mr. Rohan what was it about my writing that made him think I would be a good keynote speaker, and he mentioned one of my novels where a character refers, early in the book, to a favorite corduroy jacket and this, naturally, caught Mr. Rohan's eye. "I was disappointed, though, that it didn't come back the rest of the book. I kept waiting," he said.

"Well, the action takes place in the summer, you know," I said, defending myself somewhat, and Mr. Rohan nodded sympathetically.

Eventually, we left Gorilla Coffee, and on this past November

11, I arrived at seven p.m. at the Montauk Club, which is a grand nineteenth-century Venetian-Gothic mansion that has been the seat of the Montauk Club for over a hundred years.

Corduroy club members were told to wear at least two pieces of corduroy for the occasion, and I was proudly sporting four—green pants, brown sport coat, freshly purchased tan corduroy shirt from L.L. Bean, and a green corduroy tie, given to me by Mr. Rohan. Mr. Rohan had a designer make twenty-five corduroy ties just for the occasion and they were going for twenty-five dollars each, but as keynote speaker I got mine for free.

There was a crowd of about two hundred people, an attractive group of mostly twenty- and thirtysomethings, all decked out, of course, in lots of corduroy. There was an open bar for an hour, music played, and on a movie screen there were flashing images of Gabe Kaplan, Tom Cruise, Robert Redford, and John Ritter, among others, wearing corduroy.

One member was stationed at the door of the party and took note of the kind of wale, which is the raised portion of corduroy, that people were wearing. The final results came in at 47 percent medium wale, 31 percent pin wale, 20 percent wide wale, and 2 percent variant wale, which is a type of corduroy that has both wide and medium wales.

At 8:11 p.m. the meeting began. Minutes were read by the club secretary from the last meeting, and then Mr. Rohan gave a rousing speech in which he held up the club mascot and symbol—a stuffed corduroy whale—and people gleefully chanted, "Hail the whale! Hail the whale!" which could also, naturally, be interpreted as "Hail the wale!" He spoke of starting to make plans for the November 11, 2011, meeting, which caused there to be more chants of "Hail the whale!" Then there was a vote on a secret club handshake—a handshake that is designed to simulate the sound corduroy makes when you walk. The handshake received the necessary votes, and I recalled that at Gorilla Mr. Rohan had told me of his fondness for the "zip-zip" sound that corduroy pants make, though I have never been aware of this sound myself, despite wearing corduroy for many years. Then there was a break for more drinking, and after the break I gave my speech. I took a somewhat easy route and read an old essay of mine about an incident of adult incontinence, which I once suffered from. This essay has always been a crowd-pleaser, even for those who don't like bathroom humor, and for this occasion I merely had all the characters in the essay wearing cor-duroy, including my soiled self, and the crowd seemed to go for it.

After I spoke, Mr. Rohan's older brother, an art historian, gave a speech on "Corduroy in Art and Architecture," focusing in part on the architect Paul Rudolph, whose concrete, modernist build-ings sometimes resemble corduroy. Then there were several other speeches and the night was getting rather long and the somewhat inebriated crowd began to thin, and eventually the meeting was over and people could resume just plain old drinking, which I think made them happy. Overall, in my opinion, the meeting was a great success and a complete delight and the goal of fellowship had been achieved. I thanked Mr. Rohan for having me, and then I walked home from Park Slope, happily stroking my new corduroy tie, and all the while I tried to hear the "zip-zip" of my pants, but, alas, I couldn't.

The New York Times, 2006

"We're Not All Some Cindy!"

A number of years ago, I gave one of my books the subtitle "The Adventures of a Mildly Perverted Young Writer" and ever since then I've been the recipient of quite a few interesting invitations. I am no longer young, but I am still mildly perverted, though with less energy. Most recently, I got an invitation from a company called Metro Event Planners to attend, for free, a class they were offering called "Sex Tips to Drive Women Wild."

I decided to take up this offer, thinking that I might learn once and for all where the clitoris is, was, and has been located since I first lost my virginity twenty-five years ago on December 31, 1981. Of course, I'll also learn where the clitoris has been located long before 1981, if I'm to regard the history of female genitalia from a less self-centered point of demarcation.

There was a brief period in 1990, when I was twenty-six and read a book on the female orgasm called *For Yourself*, that I had, momentarily, a firm idea where the clitoris is, but it was some kind of high math and my mind could not hold on to the information for long. I was like that character, Charlie, in *Flowers for Algernon*, possessed with great knowledge, but only for a limited time.

So for years, I've been pretty sure that the clitoris is this bump I feel at the top, and it seems to please women when I stroke it, but I'm never fully confident that I'm in the exact right place. It's kind of like that F. Scott Fitzgerald notion that there's always a better party than the one you're presently attending. Thus, I often wonder if I'm touching the urethra or a swelling in the labia and just by chance happen to be brushing the clitoris and that's why the young lady feels good. Who knows? Also, whenever I perform oral sex it's usually quite dark and I can never see what the hell is going on down there. And then when the lights are on, which is rare, I tend to close my eyes and just let my tongue communicate my ardor.

You see, I'm something of a gentleman, even if I once labeled myself perverted, and it never seems quite proper to stare, like a stamp collector, at your lover's vagina. Somehow it's not respectful. So I sort of treat the vagina like a solar eclipse and just try to glimpse it from an angle. I do like unabashedly gazing at a woman's bush when she's standing up and we're getting dressed in the morning. I've always been more of a *Playboy* kind of guy as opposed to being a *Hustler* sort of fellow. Unfortunately, almost all bushes seem to have disappeared. I don't know if it's Chernobyl or what, but I haven't seen pubic hair on a woman in years. There's been a complete deforestation. Well, that's not entirely true. There are a few bushes left, but not many.

Anyway, I attended this class, "Sex Tips to Drive Women Wild." It was held in a large building in the Chelsea neighborhood of Manhattan. I had been directed to go to the sixth floor and to tell the receptionist that I was there for the Metro Planners course.

The sixth floor, it turned out, was in the business of renting studios to various dance troupes. In the lobby area, when I arrived, there were about a dozen women in tights flitting about, and there were three African men carrying drums. I wondered if I was in the right place. I approached the receptionist—a young, disinterested blonde.

"I'm here for the Metro Planners class," I said.

"Take a seat," she said, deeply bored. She was staring into the blue glow of her computer screen. "Someone will come find you," she added.

I squeezed past some sexy girl dancers, took a seat on a battered couch, and wondered, as a dancer bent over to stretch, if this was the right kind of place for men who needed sexual help to be taking a class. A musical-theater group came out of a studio and some of them were still singing a show tune. It was all very festive. An adorable brunette carrying a clipboard then stood in front of me: "Are you Jonathan Ames?" she asked.

"It depends," I said.

"I recognized you from one of your books," she said, smiling. "I'm Blaire Allison. I run Metro Planners. I'm the person who wrote to you. There will be two others taking the class with you, so you won't be all alone."

"Are you teaching the class?" I asked not without hope—I thought she was awfully cute.

"No, one of our erotic educators will be leading the class," she said.

"Oh," I said, trying to hide my disappointment.

"Well, I'll come back for you in about five minutes; we'll start at eight."

"Okay," I said, and she disappeared down the long hallway.

Then a man in a dark suit, wearing a black wig, approached the desk. He had yellow coloring and noble features. As a bald man, I am an expert at spotting wigs, which, as in this case, give themselves away by the manner in which they ride up their owner's neck and sort of stick out in the back.

The man in the suit was a handsome fellow, but the wig was a mistake. Nevertheless, I can appreciate the desperation and the loss of judgment that losing one's hair can cause. For years, I had a comb-over, which I was in denial about, until one day I attacked my head with a pair of clippers like a prison guard working over a new inmate. Anyway, this man looked about the crowded lobby, and then mumbled to the blonde, trying to affect discretion: "I'm here for the eight o'clock class."

"Which class?" asked the blonde, not taking her eyes off her computer screen.

"The eight o'clock class," the man again mumbled.

"Which eight o'clock class?" exhaled the blonde with annoyance.

I could see the man with the wig faltering. He had forgotten the necessary password—"Metro Planners." And he certainly did not want to tell this young girl that he was there for the sex class and he didn't want the others in the reception area to also be apprised of this fact. He muttered again, uselessly, "The class . . ."

"Which class?" she repeated. I couldn't take it. This was torture for me and for the man in the wig. I had to jump in and save the fellow.

"He's in the Metro Planners class," I said, which could have been wrong, but I was sure I was right—the wig, the embarrassed eyes, I had seen these exact symptoms in my fellow men in peep shows before Mayor Giuliani destroyed Times Square.

"Have a seat," the girl said to him.

Shortly thereafter, Blaire Allison came out and she quickly intuited who my classmates were (the other student was a happy, curly-haired youth in his midtwenties), and she led us down the hallway of dance studios, until we came to our own little boxlike studio.

We men sat in three folding chairs and in front of us was our smiling, cute, redheaded teacher. Blaire took a seat at the back of the room.

"I'm Heather," said our instructor, sitting down on a folding chair. She was wearing black slacks, a purple, frilly tuxedo top, and low heels. "I'm bisexual," she continued, "and, of course, I'm a woman, so I'm coming at this from two places of experience. So I just want to commend you. It takes a lot of courage to be here and it takes a lot of courage in the bedroom."

She seemed a little nervous. She was blushing somewhat—she had fair skin to go with her red hair—and then she said, "Can each of you give us your name or a made-up name, and why you like to go down on women?" She looked at me to start, and I was a little taken aback by how quickly we were jumping into things, so I idiotically said, "Did you ask why we like to go down on women?"

"Yes," she said, smiling.

"Well, my name is Jonathan," I said, suddenly brave, "and I like to go down on women because I like to be lost in there, just disappear in there, and I like to make women feel good." I hoped that Blaire, sitting somewhere behind me, was taking note.

"I'm Craig," said the curly-haired boy, following me, "and I like to go down on women for the same reason that Jonathan does."

"I'm Aresh," said the bewigged man, and he stopped there, showing some self-respect, unlike Craig and myself.

The first thing Heather covered was the breast and Blaire gave each of us green balloons. I had trouble tying the knot on my balloon and felt embarrassed. I've always struggled with balloons. I nearly asked Craig to tie my balloon for me, but then at the last moment I rallied and got the thing knotted.

Heather demonstrated how to stroke the breast, using her balloon, and it was fairly basic info, though she went on to suggest licking all around the breast and the areola before sucking on the nipple, explaining that this felt very good for a woman. Then she wanted us to suck our balloons to practice our "suckling." I air-sucked my balloon and Heather said, "You have to practice," and I whined, "I don't like the taste of balloons," and so she didn't press the issue. Aresh and Craig, hearing my protest, took their mouths off their balloons, and I felt bad that I was leading a small rebellion.

After the breast we moved down below. We were presented with a diagram of a vagina and I was happy to see that the clitoris was located just where I thought it was—this little bump at the top!

Heather told us that we were first to "pet" the whole area—hips, legs, belly. "Then after petting, the next is swirling," said Heather, indicating a motion that we might use with our fingers on the clitoris. "But keep the hood down," she warned. She had mentioned the clitoral hood while showing us the diagram and indicated now that one should "not lift the hood," that the clitoris was too sensitive to be exposed this way. All this was very good information. I had known there was a hood there, had heard about it, but I had always mistakenly thought that the clit and the hood were joined or something. I didn't know that it could be lifted, like the hood of a car. Knowledge!

After swirling, Heather told us that there was "good old finger fucking" and that each woman was different as to how many fingers she might like inside her. In fact, throughout the class, Heather kept reminding us that all women are different. This echoed what a friend of mine, S., had told me one night in a bar. Before taking the class, I asked S., doing some extra research, the most common mistake that a man makes in bed and she launched into a passionate, somewhat intoxicated speech: "I don't like a guy who keeps doing the same thing that must have worked with some other girl—some Cindy!—some kind of Vulcan Death Pinch that he has developed. Every girl is a new map. Girls are like mini-golf courses. There are lots of holes. There's a windmill and a village. We're not all some Cindy!"

Heather went on to tell us that for most women the G-spot was two to three inches inside, and that the best way to get a woman to ejaculate was to stimulate her G-spot.

"When a woman ejaculates, what is it that comes out of her?" I asked.

"There's a buildup of fluids," she said.

"It's not urine?" I asked.

"No," she said.

I didn't go into it, but one time a girl ejaculated on my face and I wasn't sure what the hell had happened, but I had liked it—it was very warm and lovely.

Feeling talkative, I then said, "Can we go back to the clit a moment?" Heather nodded her assent. "Well," I said, "a lot of times when I'm manually pleasing a woman, my finger slips off what I think is the clit. What should I do?"

"Try to keep your hand grounded on her pubic bone," Heather said, which didn't fully satisfy my concern in this area—my finger would still slip even if my hand was grounded—but Heather

pressed on to the next subject. "Let's move on to the ladies' ultimate pleasure," she said, "but while you're having the box lunch
don't forget the rest of her."

I didn't know why oral sex was the *ultimate* pleasure, when
some women might prefer intercourse, but I kept quiet. Heather
explained to us that while we went down on a woman that we
should continue to touch her with our hands. She also said that at
first we should tease the woman with our tongue. "Don't act like a
heat-seeking missile, going directly for the clit," she warned.

"I can't help it," said Craig, good-naturedly.

Heather then told us about licking the labia up and down, and
after we did that we should also suck each labia. "Inner labia can
stretch and swell," she said, "they're kind of like the testicles. But
just suck one labia at a time, otherwise she'll close up and you
don't want her to close up. As a girl gets more excited she wants
to open up."

I liked hearing about that, but asked, "Why does sucking on
two labia at once close her up?"

This, upon reflection, was an ignorant question: to suck on
two labia at the same time is like drawing a curtain across a stage.
Heather didn't use this theatrical metaphor, but with simple language she explained to me that getting two labia together at once
would close off the opening to the vagina.

Blaire at this point handed out peaches cut in half and we all
practiced licking the peach, which I took to much better than the
balloon. For about a minute, Craig, Aresh, Heather, and I all practiced licking the labia and licking the clit. "This is a good peach,"
I said, breaking the silence. Then I asked, "What about the girl,
who after you've been down there a long time, can't seem to come.
Any advice?"

"Oh, yeah," said Craig, knowing full well what I was talking
about.

"In that case, you might want to lift the hood," said Heather,
"but you really have to ask permission first so that she's ready."

After that Heather wound things up with a brief mention of

using dental dams, and that when playing with food, like syrup or fruit, that you should not get these items in the vagina, that the sugar can cause yeast infections. She also mentioned that you can suck on an ice cube and blow on the clit, but "don't blow air *into* the vagina, you can blow bad things up there." Being on the safety-conscious side, I appreciated these bits of advice.

So then class was over. We hadn't covered intercourse, but I had learned a great deal. Blaire collected our balloons and peaches and we three men said good-bye to the ladies, and then we walked sheepishly down the hall, past lots of sexy dancers, to the elevator.

Alone in the elevator, I engaged in some locker-room banter so that we wouldn't feel like total losers—men who had to take a sex class and then slink past young girls in leotards. "Heather kept talking about vaginas as if you can see them, but I always make love in the dark," I said.

"Me, too," said Aresh.

"So I don't think I'll ever find that hood, let alone figure out how to lift one," I said. Aresh and Craig absorbed this bit of news rather soberly. Then I continued in a more upbeat tone, really playing the class clown: "I didn't say it when we were in there, when I asked about female ejaculation, but one time a girl did ejaculate on me and I nearly drowned, but I liked it."

Both men laughed. "So what did you guys think, overall, about the class?" I then asked.

"Most of this comes naturally," said Aresh, calmly and with wisdom, "but it's good to learn a few things."

"My girlfriend took the blow job class that they offer women," Craig said, "so she wanted me to take this class."

"Only fair," I said. "And now you can go home and practice on each other."

Then we were out on the street, and what do you do after you take a sex class together? Exchange numbers? Go for a drink? No, you shake hands good-bye and quickly disperse, staggering into the night as anonymously as possible.

EPILOGUE

The next time I made love I really tried to put into practice what I had learned, and I have to say the results were excellent. I licked the areola and the whole breast before hungrily attacking the nipple like a starving child, and the young lady in question seemed quite pleased.

On the oral sex front, I then made a concerted effort to lick the labia, which was something I have been guilty of neglecting in the past, and again the results were quite good. I also plunged my middle digit in about two inches, counting off the distance with my finger along the inside of the young lady's womb the way you march out the steps between your car and a fire hydrant, and I may have actually located the G-spot, if I am to judge by the gasps of pleasure that were elicited. And at opportune moments, recalling what Heather said about women wanting to open up, I applied gentle pressure to the inner thighs, spreading the legs further, and this seemed to be a good tactic.

Nevertheless, all this was conducted in the dark and I couldn't really see what I was doing. I fumbled with my finger on the clitoris and felt very nervous about lifting the hood by accident, now that I knew it could be lifted. I wonder how many hoods I have accidently jarred over the years. A chilling thought.

Well, I didn't have to lift this young lady's hood. After attending to her labia and tapping her G-spot, I licked her bump, which I was 90 percent certain was the clitoris, and after about ten minutes she had a resounding orgasm. There was no ejaculation, but there was a lot of leg-quivering and moaning, as well as the well-articulated phrase, "I'm coming!" which seemed to certify the job as well done. When she was finished, she pulled me to her tender breast, where I listened to her happy, beating heart, and I felt like both a good student and a good lover. For one night, anyway.

Nerve, 2006

Across the Universe with Marilyn Manson

Black metal gates swing open and I steer my car up Marilyn Manson's driveway. It's a small hill, really, and there are odd, looming trees on both sides, forming a canopy, a scary dark tunnel. Manson lives in Los Angeles, it's around nine p.m. on a moonless night, and I feel like I'm in a Goth version of *Sunset Boulevard*. Will I end up dead in some pool, like the writer character played by William Holden?

I ring the front doorbell of the mansion, which has a grand, old-Hollywood look to it. The door opens and standing before me is a stocky young man in a dark T-shirt and loose jeans. There are two rings through his lips.

"Follow me," he says.

I enter the front hall and about twenty feet away there is a large, empty circular room and the only thing in it is a single white cat. Its shoulders are hunched and it looks frightened. My eyes are a bit weak and I wonder if it's a statue, some kind of joke, so that Marilyn Manson's guests can always be greeted by a white cat instead of a black cat.

"In here," says the young man, indicating a door to my immediate left. I enter a dark chamber.

"Wait here for Manson," he says, and closes the door behind me. The young fellow's manners are grave, formal, and elegant, despite his casual dress and seeming youth.

I sit down and my eyes adjust to the candlelit gloom. I'm in a smallish den and there are black velvet sheets sealed tight over the windows. There's also a flat-screen TV, a couch, a large Apple computer, and an old-fashioned Torpedo typewriter. The walls are lined with bookshelves holding hundreds of DVDs of every movie imaginable, and standing to my right is a morbid-looking, three-foot-high wax statue of Alice in Wonderland. On the table next to me is a yellowed human skull, with the nostrils acting as a pen holder for some black pens.

The teeth are rather rotten on the skull and I think how I haven't been to the dentist in ten years. Then I wonder nervously if I'm being watched on some hidden camera.

As I fret, Manson's lip-ringed manservant comes back into the room and hands me a clear goblet with a pinkish liquid. There's no smoke coming off the top, but I feel like there should be.

"Absinthe," he says, and stands over me, silent and erect. He's an excellent manservant and I appreciate his discipline and freakish behavior.

I'm not supposed to drink due to mental problems and mild liver problems, but I immediately sip the liquid, like a willing and obedient Jonestown suicider. The absinthe is chilled, refreshing, and tastes of licorice. The manservant watches me.

"What's your name?" I ask, bravely.

"Arvin," he says.

We lapse into silence.

I've spent two days reading Manson's excellent autobiography, Googling him, and listening to his music, and sipping my absinthe, I try to gather my thoughts and review what I know:

Manson, born in 1969, was raised in Ohio, where he attended a Christian school, which was meant to frighten him into obedience, but it had the opposite effect, sort of like the therapy in *A Clockwork Orange* gone haywire. His real name is Brian Warner and his grandfather was a cross-dresser who enjoyed dildos. His father poured Agent Orange on the jungles of Vietnam and dressed up as Gene Simmons when taking Manson to a Kiss concert in 1979. He's put together his own philosophy of hedonism, nihilism, and self-fulfillment, merging such disparate thinkers as Nietzsche and Anton LaVey, the founder of the Church of Satan. He began his postcollege life as a journalist in Florida, but then started playing music and broke out nationally, with Trent Reznor as his mentor, in 1994. Then, in 1999, he was partially blamed for the Columbine shooting, but resuscitated his career with his appearance in Michael Moore's film *Bowling for Columbine*. Moore asked him, "What would you have said to those boys?" and Manson answered brilliantly, "I would have listened to them. That's what nobody did." In 2005, he said he wasn't going to make any more music, but now, having changed his mind, he's coming out with a new album, his first in four years, *Eat Me, Drink Me*, and is going on tour with Slayer.

The door swings open and Manson lopes in, carrying his own goblet of absinthe. I stagger to my feet and we shake hands. His hand is long, thin, and wet. He may have just washed his hands or he is more nervous than me.

He's wearing a black T-shirt, black leather pants, and gigantic Frankenstein boots. He's six-three and looks to be all narrow torso and legs. I'm middle-aged and completely bald and immediately assess that Manson's lanky black hair is beginning to thin, probably from multiple dyeings. His face is sweet and his eyes, without colored contacts, are kindly.

We start to talk and Manson is sniffling a little, either from a cold or cocaine. Right away, he begins to tell me about the breakup of his marriage to burlesque queen Dita Von Teese. They were together six years and then in their seventh year, they got married. "It's the old cliché," he says. "Marriage changes everything."

The behavior he had manifested for the first six years—such as living like a vampire—was now unacceptable to Von Teese. But he wasn't willing to give up his vampire's hours. "I'm my most creative between three and five a.m.," he says. "That's the way I've always been."

Going to sleep at dawn and rising at dusk was not the only issue of contention, though. Before they were married he and Von Teese were never separated for more than five days, and then after they got married he wasn't seeing her three out of every four weeks due to her own hectic schedule. Manson is needy and with Von Teese on the road all the time he started losing his mind. Furthermore, he believed her when she said that the way he lived was wrong.

"But then I realized that what's wrong about me is right," he says. "My wrongness is what makes me Marilyn Manson. To play devil's advocate—but that doesn't really work, since I'm the devil—people would say that drugs and alcohol wrecked my marriage. But buyer beware. Nothing went on in the seventh year that hadn't happened the first six. But she said she had tolerated the lifestyle because she hoped I would change and threatened to leave if I didn't. I was sleeping on the couch in my own home. I was no longer supposed to be a rock star. I was someone who had to be apologized for. But I wasn't prepared to be alone. I came out of this naked, a featherless bird. I needed to get my wings back by making this record."

While his marriage was disintegrating, Manson met nineteen-year-old actress Evan Rachel Wood at a party and a platonic friendship developed. He began to talk to Wood about being in a film he wrote, *Phantasmagoria,* which is about the life of Lewis Carroll.

At one of their early meetings about the project, Wood wore heart-shaped glasses and looked like the movie poster for Kubrick's *Lolita.* Seeing her in the glasses, Manson had what the French would call a *coup de foudre*—his heart was pierced. It turns out that Wood is a huge Nabokov fan, like Manson, and had worn the heart-shaped and heart-piercing glasses on purpose, to acknowledge and ironically wink at the subtext of all that was going on—Lewis Carroll's long-rumored young-girl fetish, not to mention the nineteen-year age difference between Manson and herself. (Manson, a great believer in connections and coincidences, points out that Nabokov translated *Alice in Wonderland* into Russian.)

While Manson was separated from Von Teese, his friendship with Wood eventually turned erotic. One day Wood was licking a heart-shaped lollipop and then kissed Manson. He told her that she tasted like "Valentine's Day" and immediately wrote a song about it, "Putting Holes in Happiness."

"She's nothing less than a muse," he says.

Wood now lives with Manson, and they collaborated recently on a video of "Putting Holes in Happiness." It's the first rock video using James Cameron's 3-D technology and Manson was the star and director. The video took five days to shoot and is ten minutes long.

Cameron came to the set when they were filming a love scene between Manson and Wood. Cameron, who is primarily a producer on the video, was in the director's chair that day. Cameron said to Manson, before shooting the climactic love scene, "I'll worry about the sweet spot and you worry about the G-spot."

A few months before, when Manson was wildly depressed over losing Von Teese, Wood offered that she would die for him, that they could die together. "It might sound strange," Manson tells me, "but this made me want to live."

To me, it doesn't sound strange. I once attended, as a journalist, a Goth music festival in Illinois, and one of my chief impressions of the Goths was that they are a very romantic people. To them the chanting, the dark costumes, the blood, the apocalypse is all imbued with romance and beauty. Their apocalypse is someone else's rainbow is what I'm trying to say.

So Manson, like the Goths who follow him, is a romantic, and it's his most endearing quality.

After about two hours of drinking and talking, Manson wants to put on a CD of *Eat Me, Drink Me*. "This album was borne out of depression," he says, referring to the breakup with Von Teese, "but it's also about cannibalism in a romantic sense, the idea of wanting someone so bad, you want to devour them."

Before the album started coming together, though, he couldn't make any art for months, his misery over the failing marriage was consuming him.

"I was completely destroyed," he says. "I had no soul left. I define myself as a person, a human, an artist, as someone who makes things—writing, painting, music—and I couldn't do anything."

One day he was telling his guitarist and coproducer Tim Scold about his depression and heartbreak, and Scold said, simply, "Why don't you write a song about it?" Manson was shocked by this suggestion, but followed Scold's advice. "It's strange, but it never occurred to me to work that way," he says. "I've never laid myself out there like I have in these songs."

He puts the CD into the stereo, and I find it to be beautiful and devastating. Reading the lyrics as I listen, I think of the album as the love child of Von Teese and Wood, equal parts despair and joy. It mourns the loss of Dita Von Teese and celebrates the embrace of Evan Rachel Wood.

I occasionally look up from the lyrics, sneaking peeks at him. His eyes are always closed and the long, delicate fingers of his left hand touch his pale temple.

At one point, I nearly start crying—the music and the absinthe are working on me, and I'm thinking of all my breakups, like corpses of lost love. Then the album is over and Manson says, "You look like you were moved." I realize that he has been sneaking peaks at me as well.

Arvin, as he has throughout the night, comes in and refills our glasses, and Manson is telling me how all his previous records had been fueled by nihilism and rage at the world, but then he says, "I became so deeply depressed, which is different from being nihilistic. You have nothing to live for . . . For the first time, I lost hope."

For the first time? I think. I'm rather shocked by this. I haven't had any hope in years. Manson goes on to tell me that his depression is over now after making this very personal album and that he's more or less back to his old, strong, nihilistic self. But all of this disturbs me. Am I darker than Marilyn Manson?

I express to him that being a nihilist is a form of idealism—you don't want to tear things down if you don't think things could be better somehow, and he agrees. But *I've* never thought that way. I'm a despairist. I don't get angry at the world—I go straight to sadness. I sometimes secretly hope that man can change, but mostly I've given up.

I'm rather inebriated and don't want to think that Manson, whom I'm growing increasingly fond of, is delusional. So I say to him, feeling slightly hysterical, "Do you really think as a nihilist you can change things? Change the world?"

He sips his absinthe and says, calmly, "No. I can't change anything."

He goes on to talk about Evan Rachel Wood starring in Julie Taymor's impressionistic film about Beatles songs, called *Across the Universe,* and he mentions the song of that same title and its famous refrain: "Nothing's gonna change my world." I tell him that I know that song well—it had been put on a breakup mix tape by an old girlfriend and I had wept to it many times.

Manson then tells me that he had referenced that lyric in his song "Lamb of God" about the death of John Lennon (from his *Holy Wood* album), changing the lyric to: "Nothing's going to change the world."

I find all of this very soothing and reassuring. Manson is not delusional and I feel less alone. We're of the same mind—there's nothing to be done.

Around 2:30 a.m., we head for the kitchen to get more absinthe. It's my first time in the main part of the house. Earlier, I had used a toilet near the den. We walk down the hallway and the white cat, like Alice's white rabbit, is gone.

In the kitchen, Arvin is putting out some food for Manson—a steak and salad. Manson says, looking at the food, "I have a weight complex. I want to stay skinny. So I try to eat well. I try to come right up to the edge between healthy and not healthy." He sips his absinthe. "You have to get your body to the point where germs are afraid to live."

He pours me some blue absinthe—absinthe, apparently, comes in different colors—and he tells me that a German distillery is developing a brand just for him that will be called "Mansinthe."

Authentic absinthe, which contains wormwood, is not sold in the United States. The wormwood can cause mild hallucinations, and I have noticed, as the night has worn on, that all sources of light seem to sparkle. Manson tells me he drinks the stuff because it doesn't fatigue him, and also the long history of artists—such as Edgar Allan Poe, Rimbaud, Van Gogh—favoring absinthe appeals to him.

We leave the kitchen and walk about his house, which was once owned, he tells me, by the actress Barbara Stanwyck. The place is pretty much devoid of furniture, perhaps because of the divorce. I do spot one chair and sitting in it is a human skeleton with an animal head.

We go into Manson's music studio, which is littered with equipment and looks like the lair of a mad scientist. We also visit his painting studio. In the middle of the studio is a nineteenth-century embalming table that Manson has purchased. The table still has the brownish stains of many dead bodies on it. "I thought I might make love on it," Manson says.

Instead, he recently decided to paint a portrait of Jesus on the table. Manson wanted the death stains to come through the face of Jesus, as a sort of homage to the Shroud of Turin.

As I admire his work, he tells me about the art gallery that he opened in Hollywood, the Celebritarian Corporation. The address is 667 Melrose Avenue. "That wasn't intentional," he says. "My neighbor is a church. They might be 666."

We then step outside and there is a pool where William Holden could have floated very nicely. Staring through the trees, I can see the lights of the nearby homes. "If I was a kid in this neighborhood, I would definitely bug Marilyn Manson," he says. "That's why I get up on the roof with my pellet gun sometimes, paranoid that there are intruders."

We go back inside and Manson says, "Arvin will drive you home. You're very drunk. We don't want you to be killed."

"Thank you," I say.

A PHONE CONVERSATION, MARCH 26, 2007

JONATHAN: Hi, Marilyn.

MANSON: Hey, you got me really drunk last night. That never happens. I was trying to keep up with you.

JONATHAN: I'm sorry . . . I realize I just called you Marilyn. Is that all right?

MANSON: Anyone who's close to me calls me Manson. Strangely, I've never felt comfortable introducing myself with a woman's name. For me the name works only in its entirety. For brevity's sake, it became easier to call me Manson. Early on they called me M, but then Eminem sort of stigmatized that. He actually said—and we know each other and get along famously—when he was first starting out that he wanted to be the rap Marilyn Manson . . . He asked me to sing on his first record, and I would have except that the song he asked to me sing was—and this might sound strange to people—too misogynistic. It was the one about

killing his girlfriend and putting her in a trunk.
It was on a record I could listen to, but it was
too over-the-top for me to associate with. It
didn't represent where I was at. First of all, I
don't drive and I wouldn't put a girl in a trunk.
That's where I keep other stuff . . . That's my dry
deadpan humor kicking in.

JONATHAN: What about Trent Reznor? What's
the status of your relationship with him?

MANSON: I don't really have an answer for that. A
while ago, I saw he said something derogatory
about me in the press and I called him up and
said, "Why should we fight?" I have no hard
feelings . . . He has my former bass player
playing for him, that's the only thing we have in
common. He may be very muscular right now,
but I could still kick his ass.

JONATHAN: What are your sexual fetishes?

MANSON: First and foremost—women's stockings.
Stockings are such a fetish for me. I still wear
them onstage. I particularly like translucent
ones or skin-tone. I associate them with my
eighth-grade Bible teacher. But she was probably
wearing panty hose with a crotch panel. I also
like women's feet. If I see a woman with ugly
feet, I get angry. And I like looking at women's
shoes in a store, imagining them on a girl.

JONATHAN: I once read this great thing about
a shoe fetishist in Krafft-Ebing's *Psychopathia
Sexualis*. The guy was more in love with his wife's
shoes than with his wife and he couldn't perform
in bed with her. So Krafft-Ebing or some other
doctor told him to nail a shoe over their conjugal
bed and to look at the shoe while he made love
to his wife and maybe then he would be able

to perform. I always like thinking of that shoe
nailed over the bed.

MANSON: Yeah, you see, if I was a psychiatrist,
that's the kind of thing I would prescribe. That's
the kind of doctor I would be!

JONATHAN: Are you close to your parents? I
couldn't believe it when I read in your memoir
that your dad would say to your friends, "Have
you ever sucked a dick sweeter than mine?"

MANSON: Yeah, that's my dad. He's still potentially
perverted . . . My parents are retired now. My
mom is going through a rough period. I support
them. I'm closer to them now.

JONATHAN: You're a good son.

MARCH 27

I'm at this comedy club in Hollywood called Largo. The comedian
Morgan Murphy has put together a show and I'm to perform. I'm
a writer, but sometimes I do comedy. My dear friend Fiona Apple
has come to see me and provide support, and thinking of all the
weird connections, I recall that Fiona once covered "Across the
Universe." Manson shows up with Evan Rachel Wood and sits
with us. Fiona and Manson had met years ago and are happy to
see each other. Because it's L.A., people react calmly to Manson
and Wood.

Manson is wearing a fedora and offers me a hit from his flask
of absinthe. Having to perform, I decline. Wood is much more
beautiful in person than any photos I had seen. She looks like a
young Grace Kelly.

Aimee Mann starts the show with a few songs, which Manson
enjoys and applauds. After Mann, the comedian Patton Oswalt
takes the stage, followed by me. I tell a number of stories and do an
extended monologue on how in high school, after reading a letter

in *Penthouse* magazine describing such an action, I had put a hairbrush up my ass, producing a violent orgasm. When I get offstage, Manson hugs me and says, "Fiona is your number one fan, but so am I! I also had a hairbrush put up my ass once."

Afterward Manson tells Aimee Mann how much he admired her music *and* her role in *The Big Lebowski*, a film that Manson worships. Then a bunch of us go to Bar Marmont, where Manson has secured a VIP table.

Fiona doesn't like the scene and takes to drawing elaborate faces in a journal. The bar, I observe, is filled with Paris Hilton knockoffs, like fake Rolexes. Then it occurs to me that Paris Hilton is a knockoff of some sort. I think of Manson's song "The Beautiful People."

Manson's friend Stanton LaVey, the grandson of Anton LaVey, joins our party and tells me, "Manson is the most revered satanist, second only to my grandfather." Dave Navarro comes over to shake Manson's hand.

I ask Evan Rachel Wood what her fetishes are. She looks adoringly at Manson and says, "Boys in eye makeup is the greatest thing ever, that whole androgynous thing." The two of them are madly in love. They are Beauty and the Beast, like Manson's name in couple form. Wood used to be in a TV show, *American Gothic*, and now she's really living it. She goes on to say, explaining her attraction to androgynous boys, "I've been obsessed with David Bowie since I was five, that's what started it."

"We have so many mutual obsessions," says Manson, who is also an enormous David Bowie fan. Then Manson says, "Show him your tattoo."

Wood pulls back her skirt and right next to her adorable red panties, on her upper thigh, is a black heart with a lightning bolt inside.

"The black heart is for me," says Manson, "and the lightning bolt is for Bowie." He then shows me a black heart he's had tattooed on his inner wrist as an expression of his love for Wood.

I then have this poetic thought of how Bowie was the man

who fell to earth, and how Manson is his dark mirror—the man who came out of the earth, the suburban earth of Middle America, born Brian Warner and vomited out of his Christian-school upbringing, the child of a Vietnam vet. Manson and his father used to go to a support group for vets and the families affected by Agent Orange. You don't get more grotesquely American than that. You don't get more American than Marilyn Manson.

My thoughts are interrupted when a short, squat man approaches Manson and says, "Hi, Brian." He then shakes Manson's hand and walks away. I realize that it's Lars Ulrich, the drummer of Metallica. It's like Manson is the Godfather, people keep coming to pay him respect, including other rock stars. After Ulrich leaves, Manson says to me, "Whenever someone wants to act like they really know me, they call me Brian, but not even the people I sodomize—and I'm not saying I sodomize Evan—call me Brian."

Then he beckons me to come with him to the bathroom. Arvin materializes, follows us to the bathroom, and stands guard.

"Want to do drugs?" asks Manson.

"What kind of drugs?" I whine, scared.

"You know what kind of drugs I do," he says, and I think of his runny nose two nights before.

"I have a flight in the morning," I whimper.

"Come on," he says. "It's rock and roll."

I look at Arvin and then follow Manson into the toilet.

A few hours later, I pull up to a gas station on my way to the airport. As I pay for the gas at the register, I see that amid the display of magazines is a copy of *Penthouse* with Dita Von Teese on the cover. The headline says: "See What Manson Is Missing." This is too strange. I buy *Penthouse* for the first time in probably twenty-five years, but I feel a little embarrassed and tell the cashier, trying to explain my purchase, "I know him. Marilyn Manson."

"Really?" says the cashier in an Indian accent.

I get in my car and open the magazine. Von Teese is certainly very beautiful. Then I go to the letters section, wondering if there will be any more coincidences, but I don't see, much to my disappointment, a single letter about hairbrushes going up anyone's ass.

Spin, 2007

The Church of Surface: Three Nights in the Meatpacking District

THURSDAY, JUNE 28, 2007

I'm in a Lincoln Town Car heading to the Meatpacking District for a holiday. A paid holiday. It's a hot summer day and I live in Brooklyn and I'm crossing the East River because *GQ* wants me to spend three nights in a fancy hotel, the Gansevoort, and report back on what happens.

Some writers get sent to Afghanistan or Darfur or Baghdad. I'm sent to New York's trendy mecca to eat in upscale restaurants and look at pretty girls. What does this say about me as a writer? As a human being? It can't be good. It probably says I'm a lightweight, a clown, a fool. That I can't handle the real stuff, the real assignments. And, unfortunately, it's all true. I'm soft. If I was sent somewhere dangerous I'd probably get diarrhea before the plane touched down just from thinking about the drinking water. Also, my parents wouldn't let me go in the first place, even though I'm forty-three years old. Some people might say I'm infantilized. Others might just say I'm a good Jewish boy. Both are correct.

So what the hell. I'm not going to pass up a chance like this. Forget integrity. Forget Baghdad. Forget the world's real issues. Bring on the vapidity. Bring on the Meatpacking District.

The car pulls up to the Gansevoort, which is gleaming and white and there's plenty of glass, which makes it look modern and hip. It towers cockily and ostentatiously over the old brick buildings surrounding it. It's like the spaceship of some crazed trillionaire-playboy out of a Philip K. Dick novel, and it has landed on Greenwich Street in downtown Manhattan so that its master, the trillionaire, can run around and drink booze and chase women.

I wheel my bag inside. The lobby of the Gansevoort is sleek and filled with low chairs. Everything is colored in muted tones—gray and wood-brown and lavender. It's going for that minimalist look that says big money, but makes me think of Woody Allen's *Sleeper*. The male staff wear purple ties. The female staff smile like we're in Los Angeles. Everyone in L.A. is well versed in the art of kissing ass and smiling all the time, and this kind of behavior has made its way to New York. But smiling is good. I once heard Tony Robbins, the gigantic late-night guru, say that if you smile you fool your brain into thinking it's happy. So that's what we do in America—we fool ourselves into thinking we're happy. But what's wrong with that? Genuine happiness is nearly impossible to come by—and it's fleeting at best—so if you can give your brain a cocaine-like jolt of false happiness with a smile, why not?

I go up to my room. I'm on the twelfth floor and have a gorgeous suite—a sitting room with a window facing north, providing a view of the Empire State and Chrysler buildings. Down a brief passageway, past a full bar, is the bedroom, with a window and balcony facing west, allowing me to look, just a few blocks away, to the western edge of Manhattan and beyond that to the Hudson River and to New Jersey and to America. I think of the ending elegy of Kerouac's *On the Road*—"I sit on the old broken-down river pier watching the long, long skies over New Jersey and sense all that raw land that rolls in one unbelievable huge bulge over to the West Coast, and all that road going, all the people dreaming in the immensity of it . . ."

I watch the boats and ferries float languorously up and down the river, which glistens with sunlight, and it's actually all so beautiful that I feel giddy. So this is what it's like to be rich. This suite costs nearly eight hundred dollars a night, and I've just had a moment of genuine happiness. Granted, it costs a lot—though not out of my pocket, thank you Condé Nast and *GQ*—but the beauty of the view and its effect on my brain seem to be real, not false.

I leave the hotel to go for a stroll around the neighborhood. I cross Greenwich Street and decide to take a look at Pastis, a French bistro where the outdoor café tables are full of customers. Pastis was opened in 2000 by the famed restaurateur Keith McNally, and it's credited for launching the transformation of this neighborhood from an area known for its meatpacking plants (by day) and transsexual prostitutes (by night) into New York's most concentrated neighborhood of glitzy nightlife.

I glance inside and the restaurant is full, but there are no celebrities. At one time, celebrities flocked to Pastis, even on a Thursday afternoon. That time, though, has gone. It is now postcelebrity, but the crowds still come to Pastis, kind of like people lining up to visit Pompeii.

Lying between Greenwich Village and Chelsea, the Meatpacking District is relatively small. The streets are made up of old cobblestones, and I pass a number of meat trucks, a few surviving meat plants, and about a dozen new restaurants and bars. I make my way down Fourteenth Street and note some of the high-end stores— Stella McCartney, La Perla, Alexander McQueen.

Like everyone who revisits the Meatpacking District, I reflect, as I stroll, on how much this part of town has changed, especially since I once knew this neighborhood quite well. In 1994, when I was thirty, during a period of very low funds, I left New York and moved back in with my parents in New Jersey. But I would often borrow my mother's Ford Taurus station wagon and visit my friends in the city. Driving back to New Jersey, late at night, I would then pass through the desolate Meatpacking District on my way to the West Side Highway. My mother's car would stagger and rumble over the cobblestones, and I would gawk at all the sexy transsexual prostitutes, who, in the gloom and shadows of the meatpacking plants, were alluring and beautiful. They were changelings, mythical figures—half boy, half girl.

After months of being a voyeur, I finally let a girl into my mother's car. I'm the kind of person who has to try everything once and often twice. The old maxim "Once a philosopher, twice a pervert" certainly applies to me.

So this gorgeous Latina transsexual—I'd like to think she was at least eighteen years old, but she was probably sixteen—got into the car and instructed me to drive a few blocks to a darkened residential street, near the river, where we could safely park. She was wearing a yellow miniskirt and a white tank top. She had dyed blonde hair, a gorgeous red-painted mouth, light brown skin, and a sweet, adolescent figure—beautiful, budding little breasts— probably from taking female hormones.

Now, when you pick up a transsexual prostitute in your car, you most likely either get blown or you blow, depending on how your insanity expresses itself.

"Are you a cop?" she asked, as we rolled along the cobblestones.

"No," I said.

Legalities aside, she told me that it was twenty for a blow job, but I got so nervous about being arrested and having to call my parents to bail me out—one often saw the occasional police car cruising about—that I let the girl out of the car without even parking or doing anything. We had driven all of three blocks when I panicked. Nevertheless, I gave her the requested twenty dollars. It had been enough to simply smell her delicious, cheap perfume.

And as I walk on the cobblestones thirteen years later, I think about that beautiful transsexual Latina and I regret my spasm of nervousness. I wonder where she is now, what's become of her, and then I'm in front of a large plate-glass window of a restaurant-bar called STK on Little West Twelfth Street and behind the glass I see a fireplace burning. It's ninety-eight global-warming degrees outside and this bar, in the late afternoon, has a fire going and people sit beside the fire, sipping cocktails like they're at a ski resort.

I walk another ten feet and a homeless man lies flat on his back, sweating profusely. His eyes are closed and his swollen ankles are as purple as the staff's neckties back at the Gansevoort. In this small stretch of sidewalk, America and the Meatpacking District are spelled out—decadence, disparity, and despair. Three D's. A bad report card.

And do I want to do anything about our country? Sort of. But I'm lazy and weak and can barely hold on to my own sanity most of the time. For me it's an accomplishment if I can do my laundry, though I do try to use nontoxic detergent, which is probably a scam. So for the most part, I screw up the world just as much as the wealthy fools drinking martinis by that fireplace. To salve my conscience, I take out a five-dollar bill and say to the homeless guy, "You need some help?"

He opens his eyes and says, "I'm dying from the heat and somebody took a piss on me."

I hand him the five dollars and he smiles. It's a genuine smile. We all have our price. Mine is an eight-hundred-dollar view. This guy's brain releases some serotonin for five bucks. I smile back at him and then flee, wondering who urinated on him.

I head back to the Gansevoort, it's nearly six p.m., and I spot my friend Harry "the Mangina" Chandler lighting up a cigarette. He's wearing a pair of tight-fitting leopard-print pants, which he somehow borrowed from his mother-in-law. I guess they're the same size. Harry is forty-nine and looks like Steve McQueen in *Papillon* after McQueen (as Papillon) has been kept in solitary confinement for a long, brutal stretch. In other words, Harry's gaunt and half-dead-looking, but also handsome, with close-cropped graying blond hair.

If I was Hunter Thompson, Harry would be my Dr. Gonzo. He's been my lunatic cohort on many adventures, and I had called him earlier in the day, inviting him and his wife, Valmonte Sprout (her stage name), to the Gansevoort. Harry is a painter, sculptor, and performance artist and is most well known for wearing a prosthetic vagina—"the Mangina." I often call him "Mangie" for short and he calls himself "Manginitis," befitting his tragicomic view of himself as a disease or condition of some sort.

He's been obsessed with prosthetics (hence the prosthetic vagina) because he lost his left foot and a good deal of his left shin in a freak accident when he was twenty-nine—he was running naked and drunk down a dirt road in North Carolina and stepped in a hole, snapping his leg. He passed out from the pain and gangrene set in. So now he wears a prosthetic leg from the knee down. It comes with a rubber foot, and the whole thing fits over his stump, which is what's left of his shinbone.

"Harry," I shout, happy to see him. As I draw near, I see that he looks more crazy than usual.

"Jonathan, the greatest thing ever has happened," he says. "I got this pharmaceutical cocaine for my stump pain. It's a cream. The doctor prescribed it. It has ketamine in it, too. Special K. Horse tranquilizer. This is the real stuff. I'm supposed to rub it on my stump, but I rubbed it on my temples and I'm going crazy."

"Do you think it's dangerous to rub into your temples?"

"Of course it is. The stuff has gone right to my brain! It's great!"

We go up to my suite and Harry immediately throws himself against the northern-facing glass balcony.

"I'm going to kill myself," he shouts gleefully.

"Don't do that!" I cry.

He laughs, comes in from the balcony, and attacks the bar, opening a bottle of wine. He lights a cigarette and takes out his jar of pharmaceutical cocaine and dabs some more on his temples.

"Want to try it?" he asks.

"No . . . when is Sproutie coming?" I ask, thinking his wife will calm him down. She's twenty-five years old and a performance artist, specializing in beautiful and impressionistic dances. She moves like a cross between an aborigine leaping about a fire and Charlie Chaplin. I often call her Sproutie, babyfying her surname, and it's a fitting nickname since she's about five-two and maybe weighs ninety pounds.

"She'll be here at eight o'clock," he says.

"That's perfect," I say. "I've made dinner reservations for us at ten p.m. at a restaurant called Buddakan."

"I like Buddhism," Harry says, and he finishes his glass of wine, pours another, and takes out his marijuana pipe.

"Want to go swimming?" I ask. "There's a pool on the roof." I figure that the cold water might sober him up.

Harry loves this idea, and so I lend him a pair of running shorts and he drinks another glass of wine and smokes his pot. I'm feeling rather anxious about his state of mind, but hope for the best.

I'm sitting poolside, drying off, and Harry's at the far end of the pool, lying on the bottom, pretending to be dead. Then he emerges out of the water and gasps like Gollum in *The Lord of the Rings*. The lifeguard gives him a look. Then Harry gets out of the pool and is walking towards me when suddenly he does a pratfall, banging his prosthetic leg against the metal edge of the pool so that it really clangs. He then awkwardly collapses back into the water, sinks to the bottom, and plays dead again. The lifeguard comes over to me, with a phone in his hand, and says, "Is your friend all right?" Three other bathers gather at the pool's edge. I try to shout through the water, "Harry, cut it out!" The lifeguard is about to call security on

the phone or jump in the water when Harry emerges, and I say to
him, "Quit fooling around!"

The lifeguard retreats and Harry sits on a lounge chair next
to me. With feeling, I say, "Harry, come on, I can't get kicked
out of this place. I have to write an article. You have to tone it
down."

"I'm sorry, Jonathan," he says, and is sincerely contrite. We lay
there awhile, just looking at the sky, relaxing, and I feel at peace.
Then we return to the room and Harry pulls the stunt of rushing
the balcony again, and I think, *He once lost a foot, is he capable of
throwing himself off a twelve-story balcony?*

Sproutie shows up and has a calming effect on Harry. I say to her,
"Mangie keeps trying to throw himself off the balcony. Please tell
him to stop that."

"Mangie, don't do that," she scolds, and he hangs his head and
then smokes some more pot. Sproutie is tiny, but she has a com-
manding presence.

We all go to the western balcony and the sky is streaked with
red; the sun has died for the day. Out on the water, the broken
stumps of a pier look like black teeth.

Around ten p.m., we're at the bar at Buddakan, waiting for our table.
The lighting is dim and the chatter is loud. There are lots of pretty
girls accompanied by young men in business suits. Everything in
the Meatpacking District, befitting its name, feels crowded. Over
the bar is a Hopperesque mural with Chinese people in it instead
of lonely diners. I buy a vodka for Sproutie and a wine for Mangie.
I'm off booze and feel like a sober Gatsby, treating my friends.
With tip the drinks come to thirty dollars, which is ten dollars
more than the price for sexual relations with the Latina transsexual thirteen years ago.

My name is called and a hostess leads us to our table. We follow her down a hallway, passing a large glass cabinet filled with exotic stuffed birds, and then the hallway leads us high above a vaulted chamber, where, at the bottom, a sixty-foot banquet table rests, so that people can all eat together as if they were visiting Henry the Eighth.

We're seated at the restaurant's mezzanine level, and every table is full, and pretty girls in black skirts run about taking orders. The place itself, like so much of the Meatpacking District, is wild and ostentatious—the vaulted chamber, the glass case of birds, the gigantic mural, the banquet table, the plethora of cute waitresses. But there's nothing new in this, really. Mankind has always gone in for pompousness. Churches, banks, courthouses, pyramids, rocket ships, eyewear, lingerie, hoagies—the more elaborate the better. As a person who's never had much money, I've tried to live by that old maxim "If you act like you have money, money will come to you." Well, I've been trying that for years and I have a nice debt to show for it, but I think the same thing goes for a restaurant like Buddakan—spend a lot of money making the place look like a set from *The King and I*, and the money invested, which you can practically smell, will then draw people to spend money. It's financial magnetism. Money attracts money. It doesn't always work, but often it does. See the career of Donald Trump.

Half-baked economic theories aside, our dinner is amazing. It's basically expensive and well-prepared Chinese food, served family style. We have king crab salad, organic king salmon, short ribs, shrimp fried rice, and wok-roasted spinach. The bill comes and it's not too bad considering how good the food was—120 dollars for the three of us.

We leave Buddakan and outside the restaurant Harry lights the cigarette of a young girl with straight blonde hair, who is with two friends—a girl with curly blonde hair and a brunette. Using the lighting of the cigarette as an opening, I conduct a quick interview. They're all nineteen and grew up and still live in Westchester County, outside the city, and they're showing a lot of youthful cleavage and are wearing very short dresses.

"Your parents don't mind you being out in the city?" I ask, feeling protective, thinking of the various stories of young, under-aged girls coming to tragic ends late at night in New York.

"No, our parents don't mind," says the curly blonde, "as long we're on the last train." Then they all say in unison—"1:53!"

"I take it you guys are going to the bars. How do you get in?"

"We have connections," says the brunette.

"What do you guys like about the Meatpacking District?" I ask.

"I love the atmosphere, the bars, the restaurants," says straight blonde.

"It's cute. The cobblestones are cute," says curly blonde.

"It draws a young, chic crowd," says brunette.

I was hoping for something more profound, but why I had this hope, I don't know. Their answers are perfectly legitimate. There are no profound reasons to come to the Meatpacking District. People come here for distraction, not enlightenment. This is downtown Manhattan, not Nepal. Money is god here, not God. And, anyway, what do I care? I'm an agnostic leaning toward atheism. It doesn't bother me that this neighborhood exists in a spiritual vacuum. Kierkegaard wrote, more or less, that there were three stages of being—the aesthetic, the ethical, and the religious. In the aesthetic mode, you drink and screw as much as possible. At some point, though, according to Kierkegaard, this wears thin, so then you try to get responsible and you enter the ethical mode—you drink less and screw less. For some people this is called marriage or middle age. But then this wears thin and angst sets in—this feeling of being overwhelmed by life—and so to keep going and not kill yourself, you have a leap of faith into the spiritual.

Well, I know some of these stages quite intimately, certainly the angst stage, and the Meatpacking District is designed for those who, for the time being, are very much in the aesthetic mode. So let them revel on the cute cobblestones!

We go back to the Gansevoort, and Armand Assante is in the elevator with us. He's both handsome and depraved-looking. He stares at Sproutie, who exudes a kind of feral sexuality. We get off at the twelfth floor and he continues on up, undoubtedly to the rooftop bar.

We go to my room and we're all exhausted and lie down on my big bed. Mangie informs us that he has taken two Valium and then he removes his leg. I think to myself, *I guess they're not going back to Queens.*

"Can we crash here?" Sproutie asks.

"Sure," I say. I turn off all the lights, they get naked (they're both rather free in this way), and I keep on my boxer shorts. Since they're so skinny and I'm skinny, there's plenty of room in the bed. Sproutie's in the middle and I lie there, looking at the ceiling. She's spooning Harry, her back is to me, and so I spoon Sproutie and she murmurs contentedly. But then I get nervous and I say, "Mangie, is it okay that we're all in bed together? That I'm spooning Sproutie? Should I go to the couch?"

"It's okay," says Mangie, "just don't put it in." This makes Sproutie laugh, and so then I say, "I wouldn't put it in you, Mangie," and then we all laugh, and quite soon after that the two of them begin to breathe deeply and evenly. Then I close my eyes and join my friends in sleep.

FRIDAY, JUNE 29, 2007

In the morning, they get up early and head back to Queens. I sleep a few more hours and go to breakfast at Florent on Gansevoort Street. Florent is a dinerlike twenty-four-hour restaurant that has been in the Meatpacking District since 1985. I first came to Florent ten years ago with a friend of mine, Claudette, a dark Sudanese transsexual, who was raised in Belgium and makes her living as a makeup artist for the movies. That night Claudette had taken me on a tour of the two famous Meatpacking gay jerk-off clubs, where men would have sex in closetlike rooms. Both clubs were dark and horrific, but wildly popular. She also took me to the Vault, a three-story S&M club, which I recall as being very crowded, mostly with naked men walking around masturbating and asking the few women present to flog them. All of these places have since closed and been replaced by expensive restaurants and clothing shops.

Is this kind of change good? As a writer who's always been drawn to the gutter, my knee-jerk reaction is: this kind of change is *not* good! I'm like an alternate-universe Republican—things were better in the old perverted days!

I leave Florent and walk a block to the London Meat Co., which is right near the West Side Highway. Next to a loading dock, I step over a small puddle of blood and then climb up some stairs to an office. I ask the receptionist if I can speak to someone who can show me around, explaining that I'm from *GQ*. She introduces me to Michael Milano, the owner. He's fortysome-thing, with a compact build, a pleasant face, and a no-nonsense demeanor.

"Is the beef hanging from hooks, like in *Rocky*?" I ask, as he leads me back down the stairs to the freezers.

"No, that's a thing of the past," he says. "It's cheaper to slaugh-ter the animals and separate the parts and ship it out that way. Boxed meat. It all comes from the Midwest."

We go into the chicken freezer, which is kept colder than the meat freezer, since, according to Mike, "Chicken doesn't last as long. It's almost frozen. You want it to hold together, have a bet-ter shelf life." There are frosted pipes all about and it's wonder-fully chilly in the room, about thirty-two degrees, and it's also very crowded, filled with boxes of chicken. "We're like a submarine," Mike says, "we use every available inch."

I ask him about the blood I saw outside, and he says that's the juice that runs off chickens and that it rots the cement. If chicken juice can rot cement, what does it do to the human body, I wonder, but I don't ask Mike about this.

In the meat freezer, he introduces me to Giulio Eliseo, who is chopping up hunks of flesh. Giulio, midforties, tall and balding, hands me his card, which under his name says "Meat Artist." Mike tells me that Giulio is an expert butcher, one of the best in the city, and Giulio says, "I can kill it and bring it to your table. Not too many guys like that." I ask him to translate this and what it means is that he knows how to properly slaughter an animal, then butcher it, and that he's also an expert cook. He's kind of like a five-tool player in baseball—someone who can do it all.

Back in the office, Mike introduces me to seventy-five-year-old Norman Fineman, who has been in the business nearly sixty years. They show me a black-and-white photo of Fourteenth Street from the sixties and it's lined with meatpacking companies, replaced now by Alexander McQueen and all the other boutiques. We talk awhile and I get something of a condensed history of the district—it has been around nearly a hundred years and the high-line—the elevated train track that runs from midtown to the Meatpacking District—was built in the forties so that the meat, which was ferried across from New Jersey, could be put in refrigerated train cars and brought downtown from the ferry landing at Thirty-fourth Street. But with the advent of refrigerated trucks, the refrigerated train car fell out of favor and the high-line became obsolete, though now it's being refurbished as a park. At one time, the district had one hundred meat companies and there are now eleven left. Mike feels that the remaining meat plants, due to being a part of a co-op, will last about another thirty years in the neighborhood before being forced out.

"It used to cost eight dollars a square foot down here," says Mike, "now it's two hundred dollars a square foot."

"It used to be only meat guys and transvestites," says Norman.

"Celebrities liked it here, because it was like a hideout," says Mike. "I'd come to work at three a.m. and see Madonna and Bono. It was a cool place to be."

In the afternoon, I'm at the Gansevoort pool with my friend Tom Beller, who lives in the neighborhood. The pool is very crowded and I wonder in my mind, to the refrain of "Eleanor Rigby": *Who are all these* wealthy *people? Where does the money all come from?*

This is something I often jokily sing to myself as I watch New York transform into some kind of gigantic Palm Beach—a place for only the super-wealthy. But where *do* these people get their money? And how can I get some? What industries are making so many people rich? When the Beatles wrote "Eleanor Rigby," people were just lonely. Now they're lonely *and* wealthy.

I tell Tom that my room is nearly eight hundred dollars a night and he says, echoing my own thoughts, "Living in New York has become one long succession of sticker shock."

We circle the pool, taking in the view from all directions, and Tom points out a building on the corner of Fourteenth Street, which is being renovated. "That's going to be an Apple store," he says.

"I was told it was going to be Whole Foods," I say.

"Well, that's more or less the same thing," he says.

"That's true. Apple is the computer equivalent of organic food, but I hear that their computers are actually toxic or something."

"It's an imperfect world," says Tom.

We sit on some lounge chairs, and Tom says, "You know this is pretty good up here. I hated this hotel when it first went up, but I'm experimenting with dropping my hostility to the new and shiny, because there's just so much of it now."

"I agree. It's too exhausting to maintain a resistance to the massive commercialization of everything. Better to just accept it.

Then again, that sounds like the attitudes of the Germans in the 1930s."

"I wouldn't go that far," says Tom. "An Apple store isn't Dachau."

"I guess you're right," I say.

Dinner that night is at the elaborate Spice Market restaurant, which looks like the kind of multitiered geisha brothel you see in kung-fu movies—there's lots of carved-wood partitions and the waitresses wear Asian-style dresses.

I'm with three male friends, all of whom are married, but it's a boys' night out and we're rubbernecking like crazy at all the pretty girls, inside and outside of the restaurant. Like Buddakan, the night before, the restaurant is packed, and its large, doorlike windows are open and the sidewalk traffic is teeming and almost blending into the restaurant.

In the decadent and mindless spirit of the neighborhood, we order an elaborate meal: pepper shrimp, shaved tuna, sesame crab, squid salad, mushroom roll, lemongrass broth, lobster, halibut, strip steak, cod, two bottles of wine, a bottle of water, coffee, desserts—the whole thing in the end, with tip, is well over four hundred dollars and everything is, remarkably, delicious.

While my friends have their coffee, I approach an older, sexy French woman, who has lived in New York for the last few years. I go with my standard question: "Why do you come to the Meatpacking District?"

"I love it," she says. "Everybody knows about *Sex and the City*, even in France, and this has that feeling; it's free here. People are pretty. They're trying to be something they're not—it's an illusion—but it's okay. They come here and they can pretend they're Samantha or Carrie."

I thank her for talking to me and then I approach a table of five twenty-one-year-old girls. They are all quite cute and, naturally, they are showing lots of young cleavage. I'm twice their age and yet I stare down at their breasts like a boy in the company of five wet nurses. After introducing myself as a journalist, I ask them, "Why do you girls come to the Meatpacking District?"

> Girl #1: "The décor of the restaurants is exotic. Even
>   if the people suck, the interior design is always
>   good and you can look at that."
> Girl #2: "Samantha from *Sex and the City* lived
>   down here and she was my favorite character. I
>   keep thinking I'm going to see her, but then I
>   remember it was just a TV show."
> Girl #3: "It's just really hot and in. It's kind of like a
>   theme park."
> Girl #4: "You can just wing it, go from one place to
>   the next, just walking. It reminds me a lot of
>   L.A., except all in a few blocks."
> Girl #5: "Everyone dresses really nice. There are a lot
>   of jerks, too, but fashion-wise they're cool."

I leave the girls and think about what they said—specifically the phrases "TV show" and "theme park." In America we want to live in theme parks and TV shows. Why? We don't want real life. Real life means pain. It means taxes, STDs, aging, bad breath, impotence, traffic, the loss of people we love. No wonder we want life to be *Sex and the City* and Disneyland.

We leave Spice Market, and we stroll about, passing literally hundreds of pretty girls out on the town, and I remember what a friend of mine calls the Meatpacking District—"Little Miami." Then we go to the legendary bar Hogs and Heifers, paying five bucks each to get in.

It's a rough-hewn, good-size place, without anything notable about it except for all the bras hanging from the ceiling, like some kind of huge lacy stalactite formation. It's supposedly a biker bar, but it being Friday night, the large crowd seems touristy and not very tough. I'm wearing my seersucker jacket, and as I approach the bar to buy drinks for my friends, the bartender, a sexy brunette in a leather bra and low-cut jeans, says, "It takes balls to wear seersucker in here. I'm giving you a free drink."

I thank her for this and then ask her how many bras are hanging from the ceiling. "There are 11,802 of them," she says, "1,300 pounds of bras."

Then she and her two bartending partners, a blonde and another brunette, get up on the bar and, wearing clogs, do a spirited dance to the AC/DC song "You Shook Me All Night Long." When they're done, the girl who liked my seersucker grabs a megaphone and implores the ladies in the crowd to get up on the bar and dance. One woman volunteers, dances nicely, and then reaches under her shirt and adds her bra to the collection, which is the Hogs and Heifers tradition. Somewhere in the formation above our heads is a Julia Roberts bra and a Britney Spears bra.

My friends have a few more drinks, and then we leave as the bartenders implore the crowd, through their megaphones, to "make some noise!" Why people have to make noise to indicate they are having a good time is something that has always bothered me. I once went to Club Med on a magazine assignment and the people who organize things there—they were kind of like camp counselors for adults—kept shouting at us to make noise. I wonder if it's a Tony Robbins–like principle—that if you make noise you fool your brain into thinking that you're alive.

SATURDAY, JUNE 30, 2007

The next morning I sleep late again, and then, wearing my bathing suit, go down to the basement of the Gansevoort to their spa, which is flirtatiously called the G-Spa. I pass some empty massage rooms and find the steam room. I wrap a towel around myself and begin to sweat. I'm all alone—I have the steam room to myself.

The G-Spa is a spa by day and bar by night. I've been told that the massage rooms, when the place turns into a bar, are used by couples to have sex. Most likely this is a rumor to bring in business, but the G-Spa is supposed to be an homage to the old gay jerk-off clubs of the district—a kind of architectural nod to the past, especially since those clubs were also housed in basements.

But even if couples are fooling around in the massage rooms, I doubt that these twenty-first-century meatpacking heterosexuals are getting it on with quite the frequency that the late-twentieth-century meatpacking homosexuals managed back in the day. It also occurs to me that the Meatpacking District might be one of the few trendy neighborhoods that started out gay and turned straight; usually it's the other way around.

I'm not an urban anthropologist, but I try to figure out, while I sweat, why the neighborhood has changed so much. First there was Florent in 1985, then Hogs and Heifers in 1992, Pastis in 2000, the exclusive private club Soho House in 2003, the Gansevoort in 2004, and another thirty or so restaurants, bars, and clubs opening in the last three years. In the early to late nineties you had Giuliani, who slowly closed all sex clubs, and then in the late nineties *Sex and the City* debuted. Put all this together and you have a "perfect storm" of gentrification, with the "tipping point," to use another pop-culture term, being Pastis.

I haven't given up my suite, but I've secured a room at Soho House, which is across the street from the Gansevoort. My room at Soho House is six hundred dollars a night and with it I can have full club privileges for a day, which means access to the restaurant, bar, gaming room, library, spa, and, most important, the rooftop pool—the club's best known feature, which often attracts celebrities. But when I get to the pool, it's impossible to get a chair; it's like trying to find a parking spot in midtown. I lean against a wall and techno music plays loudly. There are no celebrities about and the crowd seems rather international, which is only fitting since

Soho House started in England, then opened this branch here in New York.

Around the pool, there's a bar, a dozen tables for lunch, and about sixty lounge chairs; there are lots of attractive women, and, in total, there are probably 120 people up here. Of that number, roughly forty people are playing with cell phones, two are reading books, three have laptops, and seven have fake breasts.

I wait for a chair to open up and a few girls splash around in the water. A fellow with gold sunglasses picks his nose discreetly but not discreetly enough. Three Japanese girls, looking very pale but appealing, order martinis. The sun is exceedingly bright and it's very hot, and I think, as I often do, about the environment, which then makes me think about mankind's other problems, and, specifically, the news that in Ireland, a few hours earlier, some terrorist doctors drove a car into an airport.

So, to me, the world, especially here at Soho House, feels like the movie *Brazil*—explosions and Christmas year-round and women addicted to plastic surgery.

Meanwhile, the girl on the lounge in front of me runs her finger up and down the screen of her iPhone, and then I see a chair open up and move for it like a gazelle.

After lying poolside for a while, I feel rather happy. One girl, asleep with her face to the sun, has unwittingly pulled down part of her bikini top and a luscious hint of nipple is visible; and another girl lies with her arms above her head, a pose I love, and I think, *This is the life.* And then I think—*is it?* I feel embarrassed for enjoying such an exclusive spot, for eyeballing girls, while doctors drive cars into airports. The world is going up in flames, literally and metaphorically, and yet here I am having a good time in the Meatpacking District, like someone dancing as the *Titanic* slips into its chilly grave.

Back at the Gansevoort, I'm having a sunset champagne party with six friends—three married couples. Everyone loves my amazing view and the sun looks gorgeous as it disappears, streaking the sky with red, and the Hudson River, for some reason, is purple.

I'm wearing my seersucker jacket again and enjoyably playing the role, once more, of the sober Gatsby. The champagne I had delivered by room service costs 125 dollars. After my friends finish the bottle, they have mixed drinks, courtesy of my room bar.

Then we all go to Soho House and up to the pool bar for more drinks on my tab. We get a bunch of lounges and the place is full. The din of conversation, along with the ever-present techno music, makes everyone shout, but since my friends are all drunk, they're happy to shout. Bowls of popcorn, seasoned with truffle oil, are passed around.

I start talking to the woman next to me, an attractive midthirties blonde, wearing tight jeans and a simple blouse. I begin with my usual salvo: "What do you think of the Meatpacking District?"

"This part of town is for people from New Jersey and underage drinkers," she says, rather snobbily. "And the restaurants suck."

"But you're a member of this club?" I ask.

"Yes," she says. "It's embarrassing to come to the Meatpacking District, but having a club gives the night a purpose, a destination, a place to meet your people. The rest are people who shouldn't be here. There are too many members who shouldn't be members. Tribeca, where I live, is the new hot place, but no one talks about it. We've been in Tribeca four years. Before that, before we had kids, we were in Soho, but it's a fucking shopping mall now."

"You're married with kids?" I say, and I think to myself that Tribeca was the hot place when JFK Jr. was still alive, but I don't correct her.

"Yeah, I have two kids," she says. "That's my husband." She jerks her thumb backward to a man on the adjacent lounge, who is balding and is talking to another balding man.

"My husband is in finance," she continues. "But don't tell anyone. My sister got me in—you have to be put up for membership by a member. She worked at Miramax, that's how she got in. They don't want people in finance; if you're a banker you can't be a member. They only want artsy-fartsies . . . Where are you from?"

"Brooklyn," I say.

"I love Brooklyn," she says. "I should have bought a brownstone there . . . Are you gay?"

"No," I say. "Do I have a gay vibe?"

"No, but you're so put together with that seersucker jacket, I thought you were gay. You're so much hotter than my husband."

I glance behind her; it seems as if her husband has heard what she said, but he doesn't seem to care.

"I wish I was single," she continues. "I'd date someone like you." It starts to dawn on me that this woman might be on coke or drunk or both.

"That's very nice of you to say."

"I really can't stand him anymore," she says, quite loudly. "He's a Republican. A Bush lover."

"I'm also a bush lover," I say, "but not the political kind."

It takes her a moment to grasp what I've said, and then she smiles and suddenly pulls me in for an embrace and I kiss her neck while looking over her shoulder at her husband, who also smiles at me.

We part from our strange embrace and she asks me, "What do you do?"

"I'm a writer," I say.

"Where do you get your ideas?" she asks innocently.

"My brain," I say.

"That's so cool," she says. "I think of planes. How do they fly? All that metal in the air—that came from someone's brain."

"Yes, it did," I say soothingly.

My friends and I leave Soho House and somehow word has spread and a wild party has broken out in my room at the Gansevoort.

About twenty-five people are abusing the bar and dancing and jumping on the bed. Mangie and Sproutie have shown up with about ten people and they're both running around naked. Mangie is wearing his mangina and some gay fellow I don't know is licking his mangina while Sproutie stands alongside them, clapping her hands and giggling.

Some people seem to be doing coke in the bathroom, and Mangie has everyone smoking pot. I had called my old friend Claudette, thinking that I should see her again, that we should have a Meatpacking reunion, and she has come by, looking as elegant and as beautiful as ever. We're on the bed, watching the gay fellow lick Mangie, and I ask her, "Are there any prostitutes left in this neighborhood?"

"They are all gone," she says. "Too many arrests . . . Well, one or two still come around, using stealth."

"What do you mean?"

"They stand by the bus stop on Fourteenth Street, waiting for a bus that never comes."

"The bus that never comes—that sounds like a play."

My cell phone rings; it's the woman from Soho House; in a moment of insanity I'd given her my number. I answer the phone.

"What are you doing?" she asks.

"Watching people dance," I say. The gay man stops licking Mangie. Sproutie gets on his shoulders and he's parading her around, triumphant. The gay man goes to my bar and drinks a mini-vodka to clear his palate.

"Are you at a club?"

"No, I'm having a party in my room."

"You're not alone?"

"No."

"I'll call you some other time, then," she says.

"Okay," I say, and we hang up, and I squeeze Claudette's hand and watch two more people disappear into the bathroom to do coke.

A little while later somebody vomits off the western-facing

balcony and this somehow puts a damper on everything and the party breaks up.

Around one a.m., I bring Sproutie and Mangie over to Soho House and give them my room for the night. They immediately make a big bubble bath and get in together. I say: "Please don't break anything. *GQ* is being very generous, but I don't want to push it."

"Don't worry," says Sproutie, and I leave them making out in the bathtub.

I then walk all over the neighborhood, hoping to spot at least one tranny, but I come up empty. Ten years earlier, there would have been dozens! There's not even a tranny at the bus stop that Claudette mentioned.

I then decide to go to a nightclub. I need to answer an important question: Is anyone in the Meatpacking District actually getting laid—besides my two friends back at Soho House—or are they all just looking very attractive but going home alone? I go to the Lotus club on Fourteenth Street, but the line is enormous and I have a thing with lines—I can't stand them.

So I don't get on the line, but I start talking to a tall, dark-haired guy in a silk shirt, who's on the sidewalk smoking. He's in his late twenties, half Greek and half Algerian, and has lived in the States for ten years. He actually works security at a Chelsea club, but tonight he has off. After I get all this information, I hit him with my usual brilliant line of inquiry: "So what do you like about the Meatpacking District?"

"I like everything about it," he says. "The environment, the style, the clothes, the drink, the food. Everything is high quality here."

"Let me ask you bluntly, then—do you ever get laid in this neighborhood? Is that why guys come here?"

"Oh, yeah. You get laid a lot here. I have a good time."

"But the girls all run in packs. Isn't that hard to deal with?"

"The pack breaks up after a few drinks and you can get a girl to go off with you. This neighborhood is very different from any-where else I've been in America. The girls are much easier."

I think about drunk girls being taken from the herd, like the weakest antelope hunted and killed by a lion—it's all very Darwinian—and then I go to a club called One, which is right next to the Gansevoort. The line is very long, but I'm able to bypass it, telling the bouncer that I'm writing an article for *GQ*. The place is darkly lit and packed with lots of young girls in short dresses. People sit on low chairs around low tables and I can see cell phones glowing with text messages and incoming calls.

Two tall British fellows come stand next to me at the bar and order drinks. I start interviewing them—they're London bankers in their early thirties and they're on a two-week holiday. One is a redhead and one is blond. They generously answer my questions, but they're both blasting me with garlic breath.

"So what do you like about this neighborhood?" I ask, trying to cock my head back so as not to breathe in their fumes.

"Trendy clubs, good-looking people," says the redhead.

"Is it easy to meet women here?" I ask.

"Oh, yes," says the blond, garlic-soaked Brit. "We've come here on holiday three years in a row."

"So you have a very high success rate with the girls in the Meatpacking District?"

"Rather," says the redhead. "It's the English accent, you see."

"It does work well," says the blond. "It's almost too easy." I think to myself that no accent is charming enough to overcome their Chernobyl breath, and as I leave the two Brits, I think about how they come to the Meatpacking District the way other men go to Thailand—they're basically on some kind of two-week sex holiday.

I peer around the club, looking to spot another interview vic-tim, but it feels too dreary to press on. I get the same answers every time. The Meatpacking District is a church of surface. They're all drawn worshipfully to the glitter, like a child staring at a snow globe. I don't judge them for this, this is where they find beauty and meaning and solace, but I have had enough.

So I leave One and head up Greenwich Street, away from the club. As I walk I see the homeless guy who had been lying on the sidewalk on Thursday. He's coming toward me and he has a big smile on his face and there's a silver plastic tiara on his round, shaved head.

"Hello," I say to him as we pass each other.

"Do I know you?" he asks.

"We met briefly the other day," I say. "You were lying down on the sidewalk and you were upset."

"Oh, yeah, I remember you," he says. "You gave me five dollars. Are you a psychiatrist?"

"No," I say. "Why do you ask?" I'm impressed that he remembers me, but not shocked—there's something of a mad, intelligent gleam in his eye.

"I thought you were a psychiatrist from Bellevue, wanting to take me in. You're not a psychiatrist or a social worker?"

"No, I'm a writer."

"Oh, I'm glad. I don't want to be locked up again."

"I understand," I say, and then add, "Listen, why do you like it down here?" I figure I've asked everyone else.

"There are a lot of beautiful girls," he says. "A girl gave me this crown. And you can make fifty bucks a night here no problem. It's pretty good."

I nod, don't know what else to say, so I end with, "Well, good night. Good luck with everything," and start to walk off. I'm not exhibiting the greatest manners, but with homeless psychiatric patients you are allowed to effect abrupt departures.

"Can I have another five?" he asks, undaunted. I think about how he makes fifty bucks a night, but I reach my hand into my wallet, find a five, and give it to him. He smiles and lifts his tiara off his head, like a gentleman removing his hat for a lady, and then he bows.

SUNDAY, JULY 1, 2007

The next morning, I go by my room at Soho House and Mangie and Sproutie are gone and haven't destroyed anything. I call Mangie to thank him for taking care of the room.

"I have to tell you what happened," says Mangie.

"What happened?" I ask, concerned.

"I couldn't sleep from rubbing too much of that cocaine into my head and so I went walking around in a bathrobe, naked, around four o'clock in the morning."

"Where was Sproutie?"

"She was in bed, asleep. So I was wandering around out of my mind and I heard music coming from this one room, so I knocked on the door and this big, tall guy says, 'What are you doing here?' And I said, 'I heard music,' and he says, 'You can come in if you have a woman or if you have drugs.' And I had my pot on me in the robe, so I said, 'I have pot,' and they let me in. It was two guys and this sexy woman and they'd been doing coke all night but were out of it, so they smoked all my pot."

"What time did you leave them?"

"Around six a.m. They kept telling me to get Sprout, but I let her sleep, and now I don't have any pot. Oh, well. It was a fun night."

We ring off, and I go to the Soho House spa, which is called the Cowshed. I take a long steam and then I get an incredible massage and reflexology treatment. On my own budget, I could never afford such a thing and I think how rich people get to have massages all the time, and then I think, *Why is it that the rich get pampered? It's the poor who need pampering; they have a much harder time of it.*

I then get late checkouts from both the Gansevoort and Soho House. My one day and night at Soho House, with massage and drinks, comes to nearly nine hundred dollars; my three nights at the Gansevoort costs three thousand dollars; and I spent about one thousand dollars on food.

I wheel my bag to the subway and for two dollars I return to Brooklyn, which is much more in keeping with my real, non-expense-account budget. As I sit on the subway, I try to make sense of it all. Have I had a good time, living for three days like the very rich? Yes. Would I return to the Meatpacking District if I had to pay for things? No.

The whole thing makes me think of *It's a Wonderful Life*. If Jimmy Stewart had never been born, then his town, Bedford Falls, would have been filled with whores and gambling and been renamed Pottersville. Stewart himself was the linchpin of respectability and cleanliness. But I always think when I watch the movie that Pottersville looks more fun than Bedford Falls, and that's kind of my feeling about the gentrification of the Meatpacking District—I liked it better when the sins were cheap and easy to come by and there was a hint of danger. I think about that beautiful tranny who got in my car thirteen years ago. I imagine she's all grown up now.

I Feel Like I'm in Saudi Arabia!— My Night Out with Lenny Kravitz

Part I

It's around midnight and I'm in the lobby of a loft building in Soho, waiting for Lenny Kravitz, and I'm feeling savagely insecure. We're to go to a nightclub, the GoldBar, and in my mind, I'm doing that old high school composition thing, "compare and contrast," and the subjects are Kravitz and yours truly.

We're both forty-three, but he's a multimillionaire and I have no money in the bank, though I do have a nice amount of debt. He's a sexual icon, has been married to Lisa Bonet and linked to Nicole Kidman and Naomi Campbell, among others, and I'm bald and my front false tooth has turned brown from coffee. He's sold millions of records singing about love—his new album is *It Is Time for a Love Revolution*—and I'm primarily known, and not well at that, for penning self-hating essays, my most famous being "I Shit My Pants in the South of France."

Then I remember something crucial: I read several old interviews and profiles of Lenny Kravitz and it was reported more than once that he only stands five foot seven. I'm six foot, when I don't affect the posture of a fishhook, which is most of the time, but if I can remember to stand up straight, I'll tower over him! I may be ugly and poor, but at least I'll be taller than Lenny Kravitz and that's got to give me some advantage, though why I feel the need for any kind of advantage and can't just meet him as a fellow human being, I don't know. Perhaps because we're not meeting as human beings: we're meeting as a Rock Star and One More Annoying Journalist.

Then the elevator opens and he is striding toward me, with a pigeon-toed gait, holding a glowing iPhone. He's got a bulky, muscular upper torso and thin legs. His skin is light brown and his face is handsome, the features are beautifully proportioned—manly chin, elegant nose, full lips.

I stand and we shake hands and he's taller than me! *Is he wearing lifts?* I wonder. I look at his black, narrow boots and don't think there could be lifts in them. So it's simply my low self-esteem asserting itself once more and distorting reality. Whenever I see photos of myself with other people, I'm often shocked to observe that I'm far taller than whomever I'm with, especially when my experience, at the time of the photo, was that I was smaller.

"There's supposed to be a car outside for us," he says. He's wearing black jeans, a black sweater, and a thick winter hat. I follow him outside into the November night.

"It's really nice to meet you," I say, like a girl in an etiquette book. He nods his head, looks at his iPhone.

A Lincoln Town Car pulls up. Kravitz tells the driver where to go—the GoldBar is only three blocks away. "We could walk," says Kravitz, "but since we have the car . . ."

We sit in silence a moment and then I say, "Congratulations on the new album—" and then I freeze, struck by my own dullness, but then my brain reassembles. "It's a really beautiful album," I continue, "I especially love the song 'I Love the Rain.'"

"Thanks, man," he says, smiling. "I appreciate you saying that." He seems to be genuinely warm and friendly, and I begin to relax. I'm with a kind person.

We pull up to the club. There's a crowd of about fifty people waiting to get in. Kravitz gets out of the car and he's met immediately by a large black bouncer, who has the physique of two washing machines stacked on top of each other. The bouncer leads as we bypass the line and then make our way through the club. Men and women stare at Kravitz and some reach for him, just to touch him. They look at me, wondering what a human fishhook is doing with Lenny Kravitz.

We make it to the back of the club, and there's a VIP setup of banquettes. There's a small group of people standing and dancing in this area and the bouncer introduces Kravitz to a fellow with a weakish chin. I realize that it's Zach Braff, but he must be a lesser VIP because he doesn't get a seat at one of the banquettes, but Kravitz and I do.

We sit down and the bouncer points out to Kravitz a loose-limbed, frat-boyish fellow who is dancing with an attractive blonde a few feet away. The bouncer recedes, as well as two stacked washing machines can recede, and Kravitz calls out to the frat boy, "John!" This John doesn't hear him, and so Kravitz repeats himself, "John! . . . John! . . . *John!*" By the last "John!" the guy finally snaps out of his goofy dance and peers over. He comes and shakes Kravitz's hand and shakes mine, smiles, and goes back to his blonde.

"Who's that?" I shout over the din.

"That's John Mayer," Kravitz shouts back.

I recognize the name and know that he's famous, but I'm not sure why. "Is he a musician?" I shout.

"Yeah, he's a great guitar player."

I look over at John Mayer and realize that the blonde he's dancing with is Cameron Diaz. She's doing a version of her ass-wiggle from *Charlie's Angels*.

"Do you drink tequila?" Kravitz inquires, opting now to scream into my ear.

"Sure," I shout back into his ear, worried that my breath is probably as bad as Donald Sutherland's at the end of *Invasion of the Body Snatchers*. I try never to drink, but when on assignment profiling Rock Stars it's hard to stay sober.

"They have great truffle fries here," he shouts. "Want some of those?"

"I'm not against truffle fries," I scream, trying to let go of the death-breath paranoia. A pretty waitress is in front of Kravitz and he orders tequila shots and fries.

I sniff the air—it's loaded with perfume, emanating from the dozens and dozens of beautiful girls.

"It smells really good in here," I scream.

"Really?" Kravitz screams back.

"It's all the perfume from the pretty girls."

"You have a sensitive nose."

"I guess I do," I scream. "Did you read the book *Perfume*?" I then ask, referring to the German novel about a serial killer who's obsessed with scent and kills women to claim their odor.

"Yeah," he screams. "I loved it. But I didn't see the movie."

"That guy from *Perfume* would go crazy in here. He'd have so many pretty girls to kill."

Luckily, after making a comment like that, the tequila arrives, halting conversation, and Kravitz generously prepares a shot (with lime) for me. He raises his glass. I raise mine. We clink. We drink. More shots arrive. I'm drunk by the third one, and Cameron Diaz and John Mayer are in the banquette next to us. Two beautiful girls are dancing in front of Kravitz and me, like girls at a strip club, except these girls are dancing for free. We drink again and I toast: "To all your friends!"

There are now more girls dancing just for us, or, rather, for him, and two have sat down, one next to him and one next to me. We're squeezed in close and my knees are touching Lenny Kravitz's knees, like we're old pals. I find this to be endearing—he's a sweet guy being kind to a journalist with bad breath, bad teeth, bad hair, and bad debt.

"You like this place?" shouts Kravitz.

"I feel like I'm in Saudi Arabia!" I shout happily. I'm no longer insecure, but, rather, I'm tipsy with a Rock Star in the kind of club I've never been to before, and Cameron Diaz is dancing again and she's not even the prettiest girl around.

And the girls come and go—models and actresses from Brazil,

the Netherlands, Denmark, Russia, Japan, France, and New Jersey. Some of them sit and talk with Lenny and if the girls come in pairs, then one of them talks to me. They'd rather be talking with Lenny, but I must be his friend, they reason, so I must have something to offer.

At some point, I meet a girl with a name that sounds like Samitra and so I cry out, "Nice to meetcha, Samitra!" and Lenny laughs. Then a Russian girl is doing some kind of amazing belly dance really close to him, and her stomach is exposed and her rear is a thing of beauty and Lenny is dancing in his seat, and then she switches to me and is putting that rear right in front of my chin and Lenny laughs again and says, "What's that look on your face?"

"It's my bachelor-party look," I scream. "Where I act like I'm really cool but I'm really not! This girl is amazing!" She looks over her shoulder at me and smiles and keeps rotating her rear, mimicking the movements of the earth and the sun, all things that spiral and are infinite, like the swirl of a beautiful girl's fingerprint on a martini glass that she puts down just before kissing you.

Lenny wrote about this bar on his new album in the song "Dancin' Til Dawn" and he got it just right: "She takes her time as she approaches me / Then she gives me the sign as she moves her behind / That only God would design . . . / The night is young, Gold Bar's the place to be . . ."

So we sit there dancing in our seats, knees touching, the girls in front of us, and then I say, out of the blue, "By the way, I'm Jewish, too." It must have been the tequila that had me blurt that out and some insane wish to have more nights like this with him, but Lenny takes it in stride and says, "That's cool, I'm half Jewish," which of course I know.

Then Lenny goes to the bathroom and a blonde Danish model, who looks like Tiger Woods's wife, is sitting next to me and we're watching Cameron Diaz dance with John Mayer.

"I wish I had the courage to ask her to dance," I scream.

"You should," screams the model.

"I can't," I scream. "You ask her to dance. She'll dance with you."

So the Danish model goes up to Cameron Diaz and they're talking and then the model points at me and Cameron Diaz looks at me, and I astrally project myself onto the ceiling, like I did when I was a kid during tense family moments. I mentally disappear for a few seconds and then the model is sitting next to me and I shout: "What did you say to her?"

"I told her that you wanted to dance with her and she said she would, why didn't you get up?"

"I astrally projected myself onto the ceiling."

"What?"

Then Lenny is back and he says to me, "Give me some titles of books to read, man, I need some new books."

"Have you read Raymond Chandler?"

He shakes his head no.

"I thought maybe you were referencing him with your new song 'The Long and Sad Goodbye.' Chandler has a book called *The Long Goodbye*. I'll get you a copy. You'll love Chandler; he writes all about L.A. in the forties and fifties."

"Cool," he says.

The Danish model gets up, whispers in my ear, "I'm going to an after-hours bar, you and Lenny should come if you want. I'll be leaving in about ten minutes."

"Okay, I'll find you," I say. It's nearly three thirty in the morning; we've been at the club for over three hours.

A Brazilian girl starts dancing in front of Lenny, and then he says, "Let's get out of here, I've got to get some sleep."

And somehow, telepathically, the gigantic bouncer knows that Lenny wants to go and he's leading us through the club and then we're in the car, and Lenny tells the driver to take him home and then me. We get to Lenny's building, we shake hands. "Thanks for a great time," I say, "and I'll see you tomorrow." I'm to formally interview him the next day, and he smiles good-bye, and then the door is slamming and the driver is taking me to Brooklyn, to my home, and I think about the Danish model and the after-hours club, but I've lost Lenny Kravitz, my access to power, and so like a male Cinderella it's time for me to go home.

PART II

I arrive at Lenny's penthouse apartment around four in the afternoon. The elevator opens up right into his home and he greets me and, in front of his publicist and someone who must be his assistant, both lovely women, he says, "Now here's the real rock star, you should have seen how the women were all over him last night."

I blush and say nothing and as I step forward, he gently asks me to take my shoes off. The place has wall-to-wall thick brown carpeting and it feels good beneath my stocking feet. Right in front of the elevator is a clear, glass piano, and next to that there's a glass staircase leading to a second floor. Behind the piano, on the wall, is a mural, a large painting of his mother, the late actress Roxie Roker, and on the opposite wall, enclosed in four individual frames, are pieces of clothing from Jimi Hendrix (a vest with wool fringes), Bob Marley (a jean shirt), John Lennon (a simple gray tunic), and Miles Davis (a strange, lipstick-red shirt).

Lenny leads me to the back of the spacious loft and we sit on a dark brown couch, which he designed. (In the last few years, he has started his own design firm, what he calls his "day job.") A fire is going in his marble fireplace and white imitation elephant tusks are planted behind me, emerging from the brown carpet like phallic love symbols. In the corner, on a shelf, I see four of Lenny's Grammys and on another, there's a pair of shoes that Muhammad Ali wore during his last fight in the Bahamas in 1980.

The lights are off, we're sitting in afternoon shadows, and Lenny's wearing jeans and a T-shirt and a necklace with the Star of David. I give him two novels, Raymond Chandler's *The Long Goodbye* and David Goodis's *Shoot the Piano Player*, which I also brought for him since I thought he might like the title. Then I turn on the tape recorder and we start the Q&A:

JONATHAN: What keeps you making music after twenty years? I still get inspired reading novels and so that makes me want to write a new novel, to try to do what the author did, to create that same effect.

LENNY: Same thing with me. I listen to the masters and it makes you want to keep going in that direction, to get your expression as pure as you can get it. Just keep elevating it. I'm always in search of that new sound, that new song.

JONATHAN: I always tell my writing students to mimic the great writers and when they do, their writing will still come out their own since it's channeled through their spirit.

LENNY: Exactly, one musician listens to another musician and you get inspired and then you do your thing, but then it's yours.

JONATHAN: What do you think about how the music industry has changed?

LENNY: It's really interesting. We created technology that enabled people to steal music really well; however you slice it, if you didn't pay for it you're stealing it. You don't walk into a restaurant and take food off the table. Bottom line is that it's changed and won't change back. There's far less money and the record companies are tripping out.

JONATHAN: Does it bum you out that there's a lot less money?

LENNY: Bottom line is I've done well. I've been blessed, I've taken care of my family, improved our lives, improved my life. If I don't make

another dime, it's good. In the Bahamas I have
one of these Airstreams on the beach; I tell
people if that's all I have left, I'm living like a
king.

JONATHAN: I have a son—

LENNY: How old?

JONATHAN: Twenty-one.

LENNY: Get out of here.

JONATHAN: It's true, and your daughter is . . .

LENNY: Just turning nineteen; she's at college.

JONATHAN: How often do you talk to her?

LENNY: Five times a day.

JONATHAN: Wow. That's cool.

LENNY: Yeah, that's the kind of relationship we have.

JONATHAN: Well, what I was thinking was this:
My son was working construction for a guy and
the guy said, "You're half Jewish and half not
Jewish, that means half of you will work for a
living and half of you won't." Now it's kind of a
weird thing to say, but my son got a kick out of
it, he saw it like he's a superhero with these two
sides. So do you see your two sides, black and
Jewish, as having given you different things?

LENNY: I just see it as a richness, not that one side
gave me one thing or another. At the end of
the day, it taught me that I didn't understand
prejudice. I didn't know my dad was white until
the first grade when somebody told me.

JONATHAN: Were you bar mitzvahed?

LENNY: No, but I went to Hebrew school. My
parents left it open for me.

JONATHAN: What do you consider your religion?

LENNY: Christian.

JONATHAN: You go to church?

LENNY: I don't go to church so much the way my

life is but it's in me every day. But the way I grew up, culturally, it was cool. I grew up between a Woody Allen movie and a Spike Lee movie, like *Crooklyn*. I grew up in that neighborhood where the movie is set, Bed-Stuy, and I grew up in Manhattan.

JONATHAN: In Hollywood, they're always saying something like "It's a cross between *Blade Runner* and *Terms of Endearment*."

LENNY: Yeah, "Lenny Kravitz is a cross between *Crooklyn* and *Annie Hall*."

JONATHAN: I heard you were working on a movie, *Barbecues and Bar Mitzvahs*.

LENNY: That's the project I promised my mom I would do just before she died. It's something I'm going to direct.

JONATHAN: Is it about your childhood?

LENNY: There are some flashbacks to childhood, but it's about a guy who's looking to settle down, he's been a player his whole life, and he makes this conscious decision at his parents' wedding anniversary that he's got to get married, have a family.

JONATHAN: There's a song on the album, "Will You Marry Me." Is that something you want, marriage?

LENNY: I definitely do.

JONATHAN: Is that song directed at one person and when the album comes out, you'll sing it for them?

LENNY: No, not for one person. But it's ready to go. Somebody will use it to propose before I do.

JONATHAN: I read a transcript of your interview with Charlie Rose in 2004 and you said you were celibate. Are you still?

LENNY: Yeah, three years.

JONATHAN (*incredulous*)**:** Really?

LENNY: Really.

JONATHAN: Are you doing some kind of meditation to help you with this?

LENNY: No, just a promise I made until I get married.

JONATHAN: But it must be hard. From what I saw last night, women make themselves available to you—

LENNY: I think they dug *you*, bro.

JONATHAN: Come on, you know it was because I was next to you.

LENNY: No, man, they dug you . . . but where I'm at in life the women have got to come with something else, not just the body, but mind and spirit.

JONATHAN: Have you come close with someone?

LENNY: Yeah, but it's difficult the way I move around. You can't blame your life, but all the work I do, it's difficult.

JONATHAN: When you date women and you tell them you're celibate, does that make them even more ardent?

LENNY: Usually trips them out, but that's the way it's going to be; I'm looking at the big picture.

Shortly after that, we stop talking since Lenny has to get ready for his daughter's birthday party that night, and so we shake hands and I say, "Thanks for meeting with me." He smiles and says, "Thanks for those books you gave me."

I then leave Lenny's apartment and I don't know if I'll ever see him again, but we had one great night together, he treated me like a friend, and for that I'm grateful. Then as I walk through Soho, heading for the subway, I think about how he's been celibate for three years and how he's been keeping it in his pants and putting it all into his music—his great new album. The love revolution, though, hasn't yet found its way into his own bedroom, but I imagine that someday he will let down his guard and the world will be restored to balance. I mean, if Lenny Kravitz isn't getting laid, even by his own choice, then something is terribly wrong.

Spin, 2008

PERSONAL ESSAYS

The Two Virgins

The summer of 1983 I was nineteen years old. I was very muscular and very blond and had nice features. Girls liked me. I was lousy in bed but that wasn't important back then.

Anyway, I was traveling in Europe that summer with my best friend from Princeton. I had saved money working for a lawn service in my hometown in New Jersey for two months and flew to London with my friend in early July. We then took a ferry to France and hitchhiked to Paris. In Paris, we were planning on staying with a mutual friend from Yale whose family was in exile from a country in the Middle East. This fellow's father had held a high rank in the government and the family was considered to be royalty, though they would never be able to return to their home.

After hitchhiking for many hours, we arrived in the fanciest part of Paris and went to our friend's apartment. At the door we were greeted by a young, dark beauty—the sister of our friend. She took one look at me and her face lit up. She and I were photo negatives of each other: she had jet-black hair and mine, from mowing lawns for two months in the sun, was red-blond; her eyebrows were thick and black, and mine were freakishly white and rather lush.

So she was smitten with me and I, in turn, was smitten with her. She was sixteen and had a perfect, young, blossoming figure.

Her face was exotic to me and she had a gorgeous mouth, as red as a new fire truck.

That night she got me alone in one of the many rooms of the apartment and we made out. It was wonderful.

My friend and I stayed with her family for several days. There were elaborate meals every night with numerous guests, and the girl would always sit next to me and secretly touch my leg. I learned that she was not supposed to be dating or kissing or doing anything with boys. Our little affair was highly clandestine and I felt like a cad since her parents were being lavishly generous to me. But the girl and I kept making out—going no further than her shirt coming off. We bought a single to make out to and played it over and over again on her little record player—"Every Breath You Take" by the Police.

One night close to when my friend and I would be leaving, the girl told me that she wanted me to take her virginity. I said that I couldn't do it, that if her father found out he would kill me. She insisted that he would not find out. Her brother even came to me and told me that he would like me to be the one to take his sister's virginity. It was all very odd. On one hand the brother was being very modern, but his statement that he "approved" of me felt somewhat medieval, befitting the country of his origin. The thing is I really was scared of the father—he was a kind man, but he was very much from the old world and I kept imagining him taking this sword that hung on the wall of the living room and plunging it into my back. In his country he had been a powerful prince, and so who was I, a strange blond Jew from New Jersey, to deflower his precious daughter, a Middle Eastern princess-in-exile?

So my friend and I left Paris, and I didn't take the girl's virginity. We went to Montpellier, where we enrolled in a French course. I grew friendly with this sweet blonde Dutch girl who was seventeen and very innocent. We kissed a few times, but that was it. She, too, was a virgin.

I left Europe and returned to Princeton for my sophomore year. The princess and the Dutch girl wrote me many letters. At some point in our correspondence the princess urged me to return to Europe to take her virginity. Then the Dutch girl wrote to me, asking of me the same service. In fact, both girls, though English was not their native tongue, used the phrase "the one." I have to say, the old ego swelled up quite nicely. Two beautiful girls—without any knowledge of each other—had chosen *me* to be *the one*!

I decided to take the following year off from school to travel. I spent several months making money as a male model to fund my adventure, and then headed over to Europe in late August of 1984. I had never been with a virgin and my whole traveling agenda was dictated by these calls to deflower. I figured I'd start in the north with the Dutch girl and then work my way down to the princess.

I flew to Amsterdam and took a train to the Dutch girl's small town. When I arrived, she informed me that she had lost her virginity ten days before and now had a serious boyfriend. I took this news in, and I figured I could at least be the second boy to have sex with her. After all, hadn't I come all the way from America? So I made a pass at her and was duly rebuffed.

I spent two days in her family's house: I was put in her little brother's bedroom. She spent the nights with her new boyfriend. Her parents were quite permissive. Each night, I lay there listening to the shallow breaths of her young brother and I felt like a fool. On the third day, I told the girl that I was leaving. I was supposed to have stayed for a week. Oddly, she was hurt that I wanted to go, but I had to get to France. I had to get to the other virgin who was waiting for me.

I took a train to Paris. I was no longer worried about the princess's father and was willing to risk getting that sword in my back. But when I got to Paris the princess told me that she, too, had recently lost her virginity and was in love with her new boyfriend. This was all before e-mail, when slow-moving letters were the only way to communicate (and international long distance was far too expensive); otherwise I might have been informed by both girls to change my plans.

But once more, I hoped to at least be number two if I couldn't be "the one," and I suggested as much to the princess, and, again, like with the Dutch girl, I was quickly rebuffed. I spent two nights on a couch and then left, my tail, literally and metaphorically, between my legs.

This had to be the most pathetic start of a trip to Europe in the history of trips to Europe. I had crossed the Atlantic anticipating thankful, loving virgins—it was one of my chief motivations for taking a year off from school; I was like a suicide bomber but without the bombs or the suicide—and I ended up with nothing. I went from feeling like a valued, golden penis-bearer to an easily replaced and dismissed little eunuch.

From Paris, feeling rather low, I headed for Barcelona, where I met an American merchant marine on shore leave. We started talking at the train-station bar—we were both having a beer—and in the way that Americans abroad sometimes become instant friends, he took me under his wing. I was twenty and he was in his late thirties. He had ten thousand American dollars on him—his pay for six months at sea—and he was looking for a companion to "party" with. We both got rooms at a cheap hotel and then headed out. After drinking for several hours, we went to a brothel. There were two women to choose from. Since he was paying for it, he got the prettier of the two and I got a very plump middle-aged woman. She had fierce onion breath. I couldn't bring myself to make love to her, and so she just held me and put her enormous breast in my mouth and nursed me like a baby. She was far from a virgin but it was a soothing experience. She stroked my hair and cooed to me. Later, outside the brothel, I thanked the merchant marine for treating me. From Barcelona, we went to Morocco, where I got dysentery and other strange things happened.

Twenty years later, I was on a book tour in the Netherlands and one of the assistants at the publishing house found the number of the Dutch girl for me—she was still living in her small town. I called her. She was shocked to hear from me and we talked for about ten minutes. She was divorced and had a young daughter. She had some kind of office job. She sounded depressed and defeated. I felt bad for the romantic young girl she had once been. We didn't get together. I have no idea what became of the princess. I imagine I could find her in Paris, next time I go there, but it's probably best to leave well enough alone.

June 25, 1983–August 1, 1983

*T*his was my first attempt at a diary, for which I used a small tan spiral notebook. At the time, I was nineteen years old and had just completed my freshman year at Princeton. After classes ended, I spent all of May and most of June working, as I mentioned in the previous essay, for a lawn service in my hometown of Oakland, New Jersey. I saved my money from this job and went to Europe for the first time, which is when the diary begins. Someday, I would like to type up all of my diaries, to revisit my life, to revisit my former selves. But I've only typed up this one and a few passages from some others. Altogether, there are twenty-five years' worth of notebooks, a few thousand pages. Most of it's blather, of course, but there's also some good stories and interesting characters. Anyway, here's the first one; I hope it's amusing.

6/25/83
8:50

Arrived in London 6/25 at 1:30. 5½ hours late. Sina's friend greeted me said: Sina broke his leg—he's in the hospital. I believed it—until Sina surprises me a few minutes later. Met Hans Olav, took him to London.

* * *

Left-hand driving! Met Sina's friends Amir and Ian. Ian was a real English John Cleese. Amazing expression. Took a bath in London. Had English meal. Steak and mushroom pie (Porter's). Went to disco, wore white jacket, met Vanessa, gorgeous blonde, danced, then left with her and girlfriend and another guy—forgot where I was staying but we found out . . .

6/26

Went to Hyde Park and Sina's home. Went to English pub, played darts. Met two boring girls.

6/27

Called parents. Spent day in Canterbury, taking pictures, taking care of business. Met 15 French girls, spoke French & kissed them. Sina's mom made great meal, lightened luggage.

6/28

Hitchhiked to Paris! Fell asleep at roadside. Got 3 rides, arrived in Paris 9:30. "Phil and Judy waited 12 hours for a lift to Paris." *[Author's note: This line in quotation marks was something we saw written on the back of a road sign at the very spot where we first started hitchhiking.]*

Got ride from trucker. Sina's friend T——'s house is fantastic. We were given dinner and Sina and I went out. Boring. We were exhausted. Slept till 12. Saw Eiffel Tower 1st thing when I got here, amazing. We were given our own apartment!

6/29

Bought train tickets, walked about Champs-Élysées arch. Spent night making out with S——, a dark, exciting, beautiful princess.

Montpellier. Arrived Vendredi. Train was magnificent, very fast, efficient. Went to beach first chance (got ride). TOPLESS!

Hitchhiked back, went to town, ate, then got lost for two hours walking. Went to town. Le Grand Odeon horrible! Met Jeal Conterrel. Went crazy at disco.

JULY

Marie Jonnyboy. I love you lots Marie, Marie.

HELP, HELP.

[Author's note: This entry was undated, but I'm assuming it was in early July and it was written down amid notes for a French class that I was taking at Université de Paul-Valéry in Montpellier. I had also, for some reason, crossed it out. Marie was my girlfriend at Princeton, whom I was planning on seeing later in the summer. She was on a sports team that would be competing in Vichy, France.]

7/12/83

"How ya doin', mates?" Tattoo of a heart was on his arm, he had been begging FAIM, gave us ride in English car, he didn't know how to drive. Wandering on roadside. Met Karmel. (Was with English girl night before.)

JULY

[Author's note: This entry was undated.]
No. Silly thoughts. Everything twists around inside my head. I'm too lazy to write, would rather keep the memories in my head. Yet will they disappear after a couple of years and I'll think I did those things? What did I feel when I walked girls on the beach in Florida? What did I feel in bed with that English girl?

She felt so soft, but not in a good way, mushy everything I touched, dissolved. Then I entered her and she was mushy there, but warm and wet. It felt good—I had made another conquest and I came.

Yet after it was over I lie next to her and only wanted to leave, why kiss her anymore? I was finished, why be tender, I had no use for her, her for me? Yet I kept kissing because I felt bad for her. I didn't want to just screw and roll over.

She said things like: "Who is the lucky girl tomorrow night . . ." and "Now I know why you don't sleep . . ."

She thought I was a stud. All I've met were people (girls) who are in love or virgins.

Some highlights of the trip:

1. Two beautiful, natural French girls named Marianne & Natalie, large, firm breasts, beautiful "bums" as Sina calls them. Tan, athletic bodies. Beautiful smiles and natural dispositions. We spent several days with them on the beach and one in town, eating croissants. We got to kiss them on the cheek! I spent one wonderfully blissful day playing volleyball in the ocean with Marianne, the younger with larger breasts. The sun, the salt water, the waves, athletics, her smile and breasts. It was so beautiful.

2. I "shat" in my pants. One night I got sick in Montp and "shat" in my pants. I had to walk for 2 miles with shit in my pants! I threw away the underwear in an alley. Reached La Voie Domitienne and shat again. I can handle anything after that night.

3. Was walking home to La Voie, and an older lady on bicycle accompanied me, very sweet. She helped me with my pronunciation. I felt good after we parted ways.

4. Almost passed out on crowded French bus, used Buddhism to get me through.

5. Got very drunk on the 13th, Sina cried over my love for Marie, had a crepe, fell asleep in the park. Listened to French hashish smokers.

6. 14th drank a bottle of wine, sat in the park. Beautiful fireworks. Everyone in the town was out from babies to elderly. We watched the procession of people. Montp has this beautiful arch and when you look through the arch you can see a Roman soldier on the horse, it was "cool."

7. Met Karmel, a laid-back listener of Neil Young. Part Moroccan, American, and French. He can't speak English, French, or Arabic well! But he loves music. Had us up to his apartment for tea and songs.

8. Met Jeal Conterrel, "Joe Cool," fast driver, but our mysterious benefactor with a lot of copains.

9. Sina became Jerry Lewis, a lot of people thought he looked like Jerry. Whenever we screwed up we say what a "Jerry."

10. I often fantasize about being a secret agent. With a bronzed muscular body, who can do anything. They call him "Spartan."

11. I am actually looking forward to returning to Princeton.

12. I miss Marie a lot, and love her very, very much. I hope it is not time and distance that is making my heart grow so fond.

Looking at my brown legs with golden rivulets. I miss lying in bed with Marie. She is so comforting. I wanted to lie with her in the park. Or hold hands on one hot day. I want to sleep with her, wake up and know she is mine. I am afraid that maybe she is with another guy. I don't know how I'll react if she makes love . . . kissing I can take.

*   *   *

I have this peculiar fantasy of surprising Marie in Vichy and having a guy in underwear answer the door (this is at night). The fantasy varies with my beating up the guy or smiling at Marie and then giving her a melting stare. Or giving her just a melting stare. Or just leaving. I don't know why I fantasize this. Maybe I want to hurt her, I think she hurt me really bad with M——, and I just don't really know it. The vision of her with him still makes me sick. I just imagine her so violated, yet she wanted it!!!!! I hate that, maybe I can never forgive her. Anna (a Dutch girl who said I should be a movie star and looked like Robert Redford, I kissed Anna) liked me a lot, but wouldn't make love because she was in love and didn't need it from someone else.

I know I was bad to Marie also . . . that night she disappeared from me for a half hour I almost died! I was crying, crying in public. How could she do that to me, how! I see now that I am still hurt by her, but not hurt enough to let go. But maybe too hurt to totally forgive her?

If she has made love to another I don't think I will take her back. I don't think I could make love to her, knowing someone else's dick had been there, I don't think I could.

7/18/83

Just sitting here on a train cruising through France. Feet propped up in blue jeans looking out the other window while French mountains and rivers say hello. I can see my silhouette and I think of my life past and future. How the past means nothing, how I like to sweat now and look at my feet. And what will the future hold? Will I remember sitting and sweating on this train?

*   *   *

Paris was good for the meals . . . and the bed . . . and the compliments from S——. The parents are so gracious!

I went to the Louvre and saw the Mona Lisa and Venus de Milo. Yet I was most inspired by the Roman statues of warriors and gods. I see how great man has been and I felt/feel inspired to commit myself to something. To feel great at something. Sweat is dripping, we're in Valence, I want to be one of those statues. Bold, courageous. I am becoming more handsome, a man perhaps. People keep thinking I'm 23 or 24.

I think I want to try at fencing this year. See if I can become good. Let loose some of my aggression on the strip, be a force.

I am afraid I might not be able to take classes this year, I don't know. I am looking forward to being at Princeton. For walking across the beautiful campus with a sweater and feeling like a college student.

I thought perhaps I would do my work ahead of time, no last second, but I always say that, maybe this time. At Princeton my life will consist of:

1. School
2. Fencing
3. Marie/girls
4. Working out
5. Parties on the weekends, movies, excursions

Next summer I would like to hike and be very rugged, work hard at living.

JULY

[Author's note: This entry was undated.]

Dear Diary and Marie, should you read this (I love you)

I've never written to a diary before, but who else does one write?

Well Diary, I think I am becoming a stronger person. Able to strive and keep walking in the dust and sun and just plod on as we all must. These last few days have been a test, a punishment perhaps. I was drunk and crazy one day and ended up hurting my leg, I was unable to walk properly for 2 days and now on the 3rd it still hurts. I have a rash on my chest and I sunburned my face for the umpteenth time. I hope I don't get cancer. Please God! Is there a God? I prayed to God last night. I was lying in bed, hot, with a wet T-shirt on my face, thousands of miles from home, not wanting to go on with this trip, the sweating, the waiting, the crowds. God, I think my brain was sweating. All I wanted was sleep, someone to bring me sleep, but people were screaming and I was all alone in my misery. Nowhere to go. I am waiting to see Marie. I know she will accept me no matter what. I wish she didn't say I want to see your blondness, I'm sick of people judging my looks, I used to want it, but not anymore. This whole trip I've gotten compliment, comment, look, yet last night all I wanted was to talk to someone. So what if I'm good-looking, just like me. Robert Redford, Greek God, Blond-Norwegian, Blond-Spartan, looks, stares, smiles. Marie loves me for me, I want to look good for her, but maybe she won't love me as much, I'm losing weight, not that tan, I have a rash in my chest, but I am growing stronger. I survived the limp, the burn is going. I want to live. I washed my clothes, I spoke French, another language, a lot today! I love and need you Marie. I realize I only need you. I don't need other girls. I hope you are the answer.

[Author's note: Please forgive, if you can, my nineteen-year-old vanity and self-absorption. For that matter, please forgive, if you can, all the other moments of vanity and self-absorption in this book, which, I

know, is a lot of forgiveness to ask for . . . That said, let me address, for a
moment, the nineteen-year-old version: After feeling quite unattractive
for the first eighteen years of my life, I hit some strange two-year period
of peak vitality and appeal to others. This culminated the following
summer with a brief modeling career in which I was photographed by
Bruce Weber and by legendary Vogue *lensman Horst. Weber included*
me in his series on athletes, and my partially nude photo was part of
his Whitney Biennial exhibition in 1987. Horst photographed me for a
Fernando Sanchez lingerie ad that was in bus stops all over New York
in 1985. By 1985, though, my looks had already begun their down-
ward spiral to their present wizened state of dissipation and collapse.]

JULY

[Author's note: This entry was undated.]
I met Ivan Goldstein. Had fantastic talk. He goes to Hampshire
College.

Met Professor, told me I was destined for success. I could do anything. He told me I was a good lover, and so on . . . he was very
odd. Went and bought croissants and sat under a tree looking at a
moon. Spent a whole night talking with L——, dreaming about
being a knight & Robert Redford.

LATE JULY

[Author's note: This entry was also undated. It is a note written to
Marie in her hotel room in Vichy, but I never gave it to her; shortly
after writing it, I had to be taken to a hospital.]
Dear Marie:
Like a fool I was lying about here with nothing to do . . . so I fig-
ured I would read your journal, like I always had. Sorry. I'm very

sorry I intruded on your thoughts, your secrets, it wasn't right; but I guess I'm glad I did. I began to cry and felt almost as if I would throw up reading that journal. It hurt me very much. I imagine you made love the day of your birthday when I called. I'm sorry I treated you bad before, because now I wanted to be faithful and you thought I didn't love you. C'est la vie . . . It is my fault, I was an asshole during the year. Yet I never thought that you weren't <u>worthy</u> of love. I always loved you, but was feeling my 18–19 years.

I think I've gotten over a good deal of my insecurity and that is perhaps why I was ready to share my love, not just to concentrate it on myself?

This whole trip I've been thinking of you. I never had lust for other girls, I didn't want sex without love. I know I could have had lots of sex—the girl in Paris wanted to screw on the floor. She loved me and was a virgin. But I didn't love her, didn't want to hurt her, leave after the sex. I knew if I screwed her I would think of you. I had this vision in my mind of you being pure and simple and I was trying to attain the same, "to be" like you—and you're becoming like I was.

You became like I was because you felt I didn't feel you worthy of my love. But when you do what you did, it is then I feel different about you. In your journal you wrote that you wanted to keep your body sacred. That's what I wanted, you were my sacred thought, ideal on this trip—the most sacred thing a person could have, a longing love; and when you tell me you made love to other boys I feel you've become less sacred, less cherished. Just another who wants sex.

*   *   *

I am glad though you had these affairs, they sound nice . . . I wish I could meet a girl like you at a bar or party.

I guess I could've, but I wasn't looking. Sina wanted me to chase girls, but I wouldn't, and he would pat me on the shoulder and say, "It's all right, wait for Marie." I would pass my time on buses, beaches, thinking of you.

I guess I began to delude myself. I really wanted to love you so much. That one night with the Holland virgin I felt so much love for you. I've grown as a person and I am glad that I didn't throw immature tantrums.

I don't feel bad that I didn't chase girls, because I know at the time I thought of you. It was like sex just to have the girls stare and point. Sina contemplated selling me for money if we got short—what a devious guy.

I guess I'm thinking of letting you go your way to be free to do as you want, not to be hampered by me. I still love you and it was with that love that we had sex last night. I hope you enjoyed it as much as with the other guys. I love you Marie, and feel like crying because I wanted to be able to tell you last night, but I was hurt, and the hurt clipped my tongue. You're a beautiful girl and will probably make someone happy. As a friend I don't advise you to screw around too much at Princeton, because I think if that is the way you want to replace the lost love of your family—I think you'll end up feeling more empty. There is no love in one-night two-night stands—I don't want you to become just a hole for others/guys in general to use, and I guess I don't want you to use guys' dicks just to fill your "hole." I don't think it is the answer for you, for anyone.

You're something special, not something to spread around, thin. Give love in hospitals, infirmaries, I think that would be good. I am confused as to what to do . . . I read your journal, a mistake I guess, I'm sorry. But maybe necessary. I've grown, matured, and love life now, just walking, seeing. I'm ready to share myself. I feel passive and my stomach tight. Oh well, I did love you very much. Jon

P.S. While reading the journal I thought of just leaving this note and going, but I didn't. I guess I have to see you again. I can't be the furious impulsive maniac I was. I am calm now, serene. Ready to love someone or maybe no one at all. I'm sorry that I hurt you, that I confused things. I'm sorry I'm such a dreamer—I do want to be a knight or something romantic, a wanderer, a bum, or maybe just a good college student. I feel clean, I made myself pure with celibacy, thinking, and some suffering. I feel very high, and wanted to carry you with me (is that all right), but there are chains of odd thoughts holding me back. Holding me back to the point of letting you go live with John, or marry Jody. Be happy girly, and don't let your dad get you down; he is good at heart, just confused like the rest of us. He does love you, I know he does, but he is afraid to tell you. He doesn't value himself and for some reason feels he would dirty you with his love. He idolizes you for you are a beautiful person, something he feels that he is not . . . no more space . . . love you Jon
[Author's note: Though I never gave this letter to Marie, it should be acknowledged that I seemed to have forgotten my own infidelity with the "English girl."]

8/1/83

Dear Mom and Dad,
I won't mail this letter but you can read it when I come home. The hours go by quickly here—my life regulated by meals, tem-

peratures, and French-speaking nurses. Yes. I came all the way to France to make my first visit to a hospital. Ma premiere fois dans un hospital, c'est la vie. Things run so smoothly as long as I am on medication, medication being painkillers, sleeping pills, and aspirins. I have never had such pain and after 5 days of it I begin to weep. I often call out your names and wish you would come running down the hall to my bedroom and comfort me like you used to. Tears are forming in my eyes as I envision you at bedside. I love you both dearly. I only wish I could call you, but I don't want to get you guys scared.

I arrived in Vichy on Thursday and on the train I began to get a fantastic headache. By the end of the trip it had stopped. I reached Marie's hotel and you should have seen her face, she almost fainted!

That night I began to feel ill and by the next day I had the headache nonstop. Sina showed up that day (Fri.) as he had wanted to stay in Montp. By Saturday I was really out of it and spent the day in bed sweating and in pain. Sina and I were supposed to leave Sunday for Venice, but I told him I couldn't. I said we'd meet either Mon. or Tues. in Venice. I thought I would get better. Halfway through Sunday I began to get worried when I couldn't leave the bed. The pain in my head was very intense, the nose, the eyes, the forehead all killed. Any movement hurt. Marie had expressed fear for her well-being and that of the team and herself—mentally, physically. Marie showed up and later in the day we took a taxi to the hospital, which received us kindly and efficiently.

Eventually they took my temp 38.7 or roughly 103. I was X-rayed and taken to a room. I did most of the speaking in French even though Marie has studied French six years. My French is good, not fluent by any means, but if I stayed here 3 months without too many Americans I would speak very well. As it is I should do well at Princeton next year. Last night was the first night I slept in 3 nights. I slept all day and feel pretty good. The food is good also. I have pain 3 times today but for roughly only ½ hour. Then the painkillers start to take effect and I feel better, and generally pass out.

I can't describe the pain—only as excruciating. I can't believe I lasted Fri. Sat. Sun. without alleviation of this pain—after a while I became delirious. I really can't take it anymore and when the pain comes back I call out your names. But I am growing stronger and do not regret this unfortunate happening. I have become a man and am able to handle myself. I feel strong and virtuous, other people will know this when they are in my presence. Dostoevsky said suffering is good and I believe him. Also, I will always try and help those less fortunate than myself, those who are suffering. I will be like the countryside about me, simple and true.

[Author's note: I never showed this letter to my parents. Why, I don't know. For the first few days at the hospital, the doctors thought I might have a brain tumor and they took numerous X-rays. But it turned out that I had a severe case of sinusitis from swimming in the Mediterranean. I was put on antibiotics and released from the hospital after eight days.]

Six-Word Memoir

I t's like my heart has sciatica.

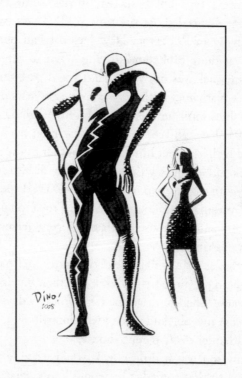

SMITH Magazine *(smithmag.net) asked me to write a six-word memoir on love and relationships.*

Two Diary Entries About My Son

So before I type up these two entries, some explaining, I imagine, is needed. At the time, 1991, I was twenty-seven and living in Princeton, New Jersey. I had published one novel, but was quite broke and driving a taxi to support myself. My son, Nathaniel, was five years old. I was a part-time dad, and I didn't meet Nathaniel until he was over two years old. (I didn't know about him until he was fifteen months old—a long story.) Back in 1991, I would see him every few months; I'd fly down south where he lives, meet him and his mother in the airport, and then fly back to New Jersey that same day with him in tow. He'd usually stay with me for two or three weeks. We'd spend some of the time in my small studio apartment in Princeton and some of the time at my parents' house in Oakland, New Jersey, about two hours north of Princeton.

This particular visit, which the entries refer to, I had him with me in Princeton for more than a week and then my dad came and got him because I had to drive the taxi for a few days and nights so as not to lose my job. And when I was done driving, I was going to rejoin Nathaniel at my parents' house.

When my son was a little boy, I would write letters to him in my journal so that someday he would know what he was like and what we had done together; the second entry is one of these letters. I think that's enough explaining. Wait, maybe two more things—in my journals I use a lot of ellipses, and in Princeton, as a cab driver, you wait a lot in your car at the taxi stand, hoping for a fare, so I was able to write in my journal as I sat there, which explains the second entry.

12/12/91

TWA, in the air, over Virginia, or some such southern state.

Nathaniel is next to me beautiful and big, drawing; he's given his Transformers to the boy behind us to play with . . .

When he saw me in the airport he came running and leaped into my arms, a smile bursting the whole way!! God what more could a human being want. It's good to put my hands in his hair, he's really grown; we have the same hands, his eyelashes are long . . . He's making letters, singing to himself. Future Nathaniel, know in this moment that I truly admire you and love you. I wish I was with you more . . . have to get out of debt and move down south . . . write to colleges there and get a teaching job . . . wear my seersucker jacket around some campus . . . be with my son. My son. Are you my real dad? he says . . . Yes, I say, of course I am. If you're my real dad you should live with me . . . Well, he knows I'm his dad . . . so far everything's o.k. I got out of Princeton this morning up at 5:45, jacket, tie, sweater-vest for my son . . . we'll have fun together, adventures, I'm looking forward to it. Well, this little journal, well I was going to close it, but there are two pages left.

[Then I wrote a summary of what the journal had seen, too abstract to include here. Picking it up again, still on the plane:]

Feels good to write, to let Nathaniel be, don't have to play with him constantly as I have in the past, love having him near me . . . take him anywhere . . . it was nice being in the car with my father today, he was telling me his woes, his fears: retire? go on social security? . . . I enjoyed listening, but the roles did feel reversed. Could I have told him my problems, what a financial mess I'm in?

Nathaniel did a great drawing of a plane . . . I drank two cups of coffee . . . my armpits stink from too much sweating . . . two flights, one day . . . I'll finish this journal soon.

[There was one page left, which was filled with the following entry.]

12/20/91

Dear Future Nathaniel,

Some sad jazz is playing on the radio, just simple lonely piano, and that's how I feel sitting here in my taxi.

It's night, a full moon in the somewhat hazy black sky.

I just called you and you didn't sound happy to hear from me . . . and we were together eight straight days, morning, noon, and night, and who knows how many times I zipped your coat, and towards the end I was losing patience . . . please forgive me, we were cooped up in my room . . . you already put yourself down and then I give you a hard time, and you want, want, want, and even if I had money I couldn't give you all that you fleetingly "I WANT . . ."

So we parted today on a sour note . . . (Grandpa picked you up . . .) You had trouble sleeping last night, I read you extra stories, and sang to you again and again and then you woke up coughing for hours and I lay awake, unable to sleep, you slept and coughed, I prayed to God for patience, for love, for you to stop coughing; a lot of times I can't wait for you to be a man so that I can explain to you that I hadn't meant to be a dad, and that I'm still all confused and broken up inside . . . I'm running out of space, I have to go, my first job of the night. I'm back, two jobs, no tips . . . but 14.50 for me in one hour . . . So Nathaniel, when you saw me in the airport you came running, bursting with a smile, you leapt into my arms . . . you are beautiful . . . I do love you. I'm doing the best I can. God please help me. The end.

[Then scrawled along the edge:]
P.S. You liked Waldo books, you started learning how to fence, we went to NY . . . lots of things. No more room.

The Failed Comb-over

Several years ago, when I was in my midthirties, I attended a writer's conference at a small southwestern university. One of the students—not in my class—began to spend time with me. She had just graduated college and was exceedingly lovely, with very long blonde hair that went all the way to her waist. We would only make out when we went for walks in the woods near the university, but then on the last night of the conference we snuck her into my room (we both didn't want people gossiping). I was in the midst of a drinking relapse and was quite intoxicated. We got naked and eventually I put on a condom and tried to get it in her, but couldn't. She was very tight and I was very tight (drunk, that is). I had gone down on her, so she was wet enough, but she was too tight, and with all the booze in my system, my erection started to wilt when it wasn't given easy access. Then, somehow, I got my semihard penis in there, and I think my penis was so relieved to have made it inside that it let down its guard, spazzed out, and prematurely ejaculated.

This was terribly embarrassing, so I went down on her again for some time to compensate for my lousy lovemaking and eventually we both fell asleep. She left my room in the wee hours of the morning and when I woke up a little while later and went to the bathroom I saw that my face was a mask of blood. At first I thought something had happened to me, that I had put my face through a window in my drunkenness, but then I realized that the girl had started her period and when I went down on her the second time my face had gotten covered. I recalled that she had been very wet, but I had thought it was just her natural effusion. Also, the room had been very dark, so I hadn't perceived the blood and in my intoxicated state I hadn't discerned the taste of it. Somewhat disturbed, I washed off the dried blood. What a strange night it had been, and I figured she hadn't said anything when she left, probably out of embarrassment.

Anyway, the conference broke up later that morning and the girl and I parted sweetly. Naturally, I didn't say anything about her having her period all over my face, and, anyway, I was more embarrassed and upset about my bad lovemaking skills than about her menstruating on me.

About a month later, she moved to New York, contacted me, and we ended up in bed. We were naked and just getting into things when she said, "I have something to tell you." I figured she was going to confess to me about having her period that night and that she was sorry she had bled all over me. So she took a deep breath and said, "When we had sex a month ago . . . well, I was a virgin. That was my first time. I'm sorry I didn't say anything then."

I was flabbergasted to say the least. I couldn't believe that her first time had been with a drunken, prematurely ejaculating idiot. I was so embarrassed. Also, she was the first virgin I had ever been with and I hadn't even known it! No wonder she had been so hard to penetrate, and my face, I realized, had been painted with the blood of her broken hymen!

"Why me?" I asked.

"Because you're old, and I figured you would know what to do, and for some reason I got it in my head that I should lose my virginity with someone that I can't have a relationship with."

"Why can't you have a relationship with me?" I asked.

"You're too old," she said. "But we can have sex."

That seemed fair enough, and boy, did I put in a Herculean effort that night to make up for what had transpired a month before. She left late the next morning and about an hour after she was gone the doorbell rang. I went to the front door and it was my ex, who had broken up with me two months earlier and whom I had been pining for (hence the drinking relapse at the conference). But she had finally returned! She came up to my apartment and said, "I've been calling you all night and all morning."

"My phone has been off," I said, which it had been since I was with the other girl. My ex bought this explanation and with hardly another word exchanged between us, she stripped off her clothes. I rallied to the cause and performed admirably. When it was over, we were lying there rather happily, but then she located a very long blonde hair on my pillow. My ex, I should mention, had short black hair.

"What's this?" she said, quite accusingly.

At the time, I had thinning blond hair, which was styled in that classic configuration known as the comb-over. I took the hair from her and said, "It's mine," and I proceeded to drape the hair from my left ear to my right, fitting it in with the other comb-over strands, except the hair kept going—it went from my left ear all the way to my right hip!

"That's why you didn't answer your phone," she shouted. "You had someone here last night! This is disgusting! I think I'm going to throw up!"

She then leaped out of my bed, got dressed faster than I've ever seen a woman dress, and ran out of the apartment and, ultimately, out of my life, and I was heartbroken. I did try racing after her in my slippers that day, but it was futile, as were my subsequent phone calls and pleas.

As a slight compensation, the ex-virgin slept with me two more times, but then found a boyfriend closer to her age and that was that.

Nerve, 2006

Another Six-Word Memoir

All my relationships end in pain.

A Brief Foreword for Reverend Jen's
Live Nude Elf

I am Rev Jen's literary agent, former lover, and ever-passionate admirer. In my humble opinion, she is one of the most remarkable human beings I've ever met. She is such a great artist that she *is* art. Her life is art. But this doesn't mean that she's just some mad eccentric. Well, she is a mad eccentric, but she is also a wildly productive artist: she makes gorgeous paintings; she writes essays, fiction, plays, television shows, puppet shows, and screenplays; she builds props and stage sets; she manages a Troll museum; she publishes and edits *A.S.S. Magazine*, which she founded; she performs as an actress, storyteller, comedienne, and author; she makes art books and objects that have been displayed in museums; she hosts a monthly open-mike performance show called Rev Jen's Anti-Slam, which has been going strong for twelve years; she directs her plays, movies, and television shows. Essentially, she's a Picasso-like force of nature.

There's a performance-art scene in New York City that she has helped create, and the players in the scene are called Art Stars. They're the freakiest, most dysfunctional band of incredible lunatics, shining and exploding luminescently like human Northern Lights. No one has money, everyone barely gets by, the sexualities are as diverse as the insect world, and they all indefatigably produce the most outrageous performances, unparalleled in their creativity, humor, and beauty. They're a wild mix of comedians, singers, sketch artists, poets, and soap-box ranters. Rev Jen came up with the term "Art Stars," in much the same way that Jack Kerouac coined the term "Beats," and in the scene, she's like the prime minister—she's Frank Sinatra, Mae West, Emma Peel, and Galadriel, all in one. She is beloved.

Now let's talk about her person. She's kind, humble, and forgiving. She drinks too much beer and she wears elf ears all the time. Her relationships with men (except for those who become her literary agent) are tormented and deranged. She barely gets by and has to work as a sexual surrogate to support herself, which means that she masturbates men who go to a psychiatrist for a variety of sexual problems. Her dearest companion is her dog, a feisty and elegant chihuahua named Rev Jen Jr., who attends every show of the Art Stars, barking out her displeasure or her joy.

So that's something of a snapshot of my dear friend; it's not nearly voluminous enough, but I hope it gives you some idea of the extraordinary and unique author you are about to engage. I won't try to explain this book that you are holding; it can speak for itself and beautifully at that. I do think you will love it and come to love Rev Jen as well. I know I do.

This is the foreword I wrote for Live Nude Elf: The Sexperiments of Reverend Jen. *It was published in 2009 by Soft Skull Press. I am, indeed, her literary agent and she is my sole client. It should also be noted that Rev Jen writes and directs a serial play called* Reverend Jen's Really Cool Neighborhood, *and a new episode is performed every few months. Sometimes these episodes are filmed. So it's half movie and half stage-play, and my friend Mangina is a recurring character. He plays a naked postman, delivering odd packages, while wearing his mangina and an old-fashioned postal cap. His rugged, Henry Fonda looks make him ideal for this role. In one episode, Rev Jen and Mangina get drunk and black out but have sex for the first and only time. In a later episode, Mangina, not remembering this sexual encounter and thinking it was some kind of immaculate conception, discovers that he's pregnant and then gives birth to a baby boy—me. At the Bowery Poetry Club, during a performance of this episode, I was hidden under a table and then emerged from between his legs, wearing only boxer shorts and swim-goggles. My body was covered in vegan Jell-O and I came out of his womb, mewling and howling in pain. Life, after all, is very painful. He then took me to his breast and soothed me, while Rev Jen, my father in this instance, looked on. For more info on Rev Jen go to* www.revjen.com.

A Glorious Baptism

Several years ago, I had a brief affair with a young, very attractive brunette. She had a full figure and was a fan of my writing. She contacted me via e-mail and included a rather fetching photograph of herself. After a few e-mails, we progressed to talking on the phone and then we got together at a bar. She had a few drinks and then she leaned forward and kissed me. It was a nice kiss and I was feeling rather happy, and then she said to me, "I figured that from your writing you were some kind of male slut and that it would be easy to sleep with you."

One doesn't like to hear the truth spoken so nakedly, and I wanted to protest this statement, but simply uttered, noncommittally, "Male slut?!?"

We fooled around, by my estimation, six times. The first two dates, we simply made out. On the third date, we ended up in bed, but didn't have intercourse. I did go down on her, though, and noticed something curious: right when she seemed on the verge of climax, she would make me stop. This happened a few times and I didn't question her about it. I figured that coming would make her feel vulnerable and she wasn't ready for that.

On our fourth and fifth dates, the same thing happened, though. Either by hand or mouth, I would bring her very close, seemingly, to orgasm, but she would always halt the proceedings. Eventually, on the fifth date, I gently inquired, "Is everything okay? Why don't you want to come?" She mumbled something about not wanting to lose control, and this, I thought, confirmed my initial hypothesis, so I didn't press the issue.

The sixth time we were in bed, since she seemed to enjoy it for the most part, I went down on her, but, as usual, she wouldn't allow herself to have an orgasm. We made love, though, for the first time that night and it was quite nice. She didn't come, but I didn't think she would.

After lying there, postcoitally, for about twenty minutes, I felt inspired and went back down on her. Something had changed—she wasn't stopping me every few minutes. The love-making seemed to have relaxed her, so I was happily licking away and an orgasm seemed to be approaching—she was pushing against my tongue with great urgency and she wasn't stopping!

Then, suddenly, she convulsed and there was a gush of warm liquid into my face that would not stop. I'm not joking when I say that I felt like I was drowning, but I kept on licking through this rainstorm as she thrashed about wildly. At first I thought she was urinating on me while orgasming, but then, though I was in a state of shock, it dawned on me that I was experiencing—as an observer and recipient—the first vaginal ejaculation of my life!

I had long heard rumors about such a phenomenon—to my mind, it was kind of a sexual Loch Ness monster and I had always felt somewhat incredulous. But now there was no denying the empirical evidence of the geyser that was shooting into my face.

Maybe because I was having a near-death experience, seconds felt like minutes as I drowned and licked. Then her tremors subsided, and I could breathe and there was a hush in the air, a calming peace. The atmosphere was not unlike the quiet that follows a great storm.

I washed up between her thighs, my face resting in a substantial puddle on my sheets. I now knew why she had always kept herself from coming. If each orgasm was like putting a pin in a hot-water bottle, I could fully understand not wanting to have such a thing happen until you felt comfortable with your partner.

So I happily lay in that puddle, sort of reveling in the newness of it all, but not wanting to embarrass her, I eventually wiped my face on a dry bit of sheet and crawled up next to her. I held her from behind and we lay there silently, not speaking about what had just happened. Then we both fell into a deep, pleasing slumber.

It's rather complicated to go into, but after that night I never saw her again. Subsequently, a few years later, I met a girl whose vagina seemed to hiccup when she came and a little bit of liquid would be released—my second female ejaculator—but I've never again had such a glorious baptism as I did that one night. I do wonder what became of that girl. I have to say that I'd love to see her again.

This was written for an anthology, Dirty Words: A Literary Encyclopedia of Sex *(Bloomsbury 2008). Writers were asked to select a word or phrase from a very extensive list—I chose 'vaginal ejaculation'—and then define that word or phrase however we saw fit.*

E-mail Re: Mangina

*H*ere is an e-mail I wrote to a few close friends that is fairly self-explanatory. The event in question—a night of strange performance art—took place in a tiny theater in the East Village for an audience of about eleven people. Amy Uzi, mentioned below—full name Ouzoonian—was the impresario of the show. The friends I wrote to often call me "herring," a shortened version of my fight name, "The Herring Wonder," and I usually sign my e-mails to this group of friends with "Herring" instead of "Jonathan," but for this note, as you can see, I slightly changed my nickname at the end of the e-mail. Also, when I write e-mails, I only use the lower-case for reasons of expediency. One other thing: my friend Harry "the Mangina" Chandler, who was part of this performance,

was wearing a full-body stocking, mangina, a garish red wig that he flung off, and horrific blood-red lipstick. To see a photograph of this event, go to http://farm4.static.flickr.com/3226/2521139941_2acbe090a9_b.jpg.

dear friends,

last night mangina and i had our greatest and yet most terrible performance ever.

i was to be the ref of a wrestling match of mangina vs. some girl. well, he body-slammed the girl and then took his foot off and she ran into the audience, and then he, hopping around on one foot, somehow knocked me down (he was hitting me over the head viciously with his rubber stump-sock/shock absorber thing and it gives off a terrible odor, like the inside of a thousand pairs of old sneakers, and the smell weakened me, it's like an amazonian toad squirting you with some paralyzing poison before ingesting you . . .) and then once i was down, paralyzed by the stump odor, he used his superhuman mangina strength and literally—i'm not kidding—ripped my pants off of me, shredding my underwear, and got his stump between my legs and against my anus and he began to thrust like a serial killer/ rabid dog. he was completely deranged. i was kicking him in the chest, trying to get him off me, but he was hell-bent on penetration. amy uzi tried to break it up and may have saved me from having my anus ripped . . . mangina went completely off his rocker . . . somehow uzi did manage to get him off me and i crawled away and then limped offstage, my ass showing to the audience through my shredded boxers, and my jeans were at my knees . . .

later mangina rushed the audience and violently fingered himself and the show was over . . .

it was beyond punk rock. it was like a prison rape by a tranny clown.

filleted herring

Why Did I Write *The Alcoholic*?

Well, there are a number of reasons, but, mostly, I did it out of friendship. About seven years ago, I was sitting in a café in Brooklyn. The kind with torn-up couches and maybe one cute girl writing something on a computer. So I was having a coffee and feeling a little lonely. Then this guy came up to me, said he was a fan of my writing. He was cocky and full of life and he went on to say that he illustrated comics and that we should hang out sometime. His name was Dean Haspiel. I'm a loner and don't have many friends, but somehow Dean became my friend.

As time went on, Dean kept saying we should collaborate. I'm a Charles Bukowski fan and I loved how R. Crumb had illustrated some of Bukowski's stories and I thought maybe Dean and I could do something along those lines. Then Dean gave me a bunch of issues of *Y: The Last Man* and I really got into it. I suddenly had this idea for a six-part comic about an alcoholic on a bender—after a young girl breaks his heart—and that each issue would end with a cliffhanger, like in *Y*. One issue we'd see "the alcoholic" hanging from a fire escape, so people would have to wait a month to see what happens, and the next issue it would end with him running down a street naked, and so on.

Well, this idea morphed into a graphic novel, *The Alcoholic*, which is essentially a life story as one big bender, and so there are plenty of girls and fights and madness and heartbreak. I based the character somewhat on myself, calling him "Jonathan A.," with the idea that the "A." could stand for "alcoholic" or "alone" or "Ames." In effect, I created a doppelgänger for myself, which enabled me to write about things I hadn't yet explored in my novels, like what happened to me in New York City on 9/11. So the book is a mixture of comedy and tragedy, kind of like an alcoholic—you start off laughing, enjoying your drinks, and then things can turn dark, which keeps in place my original idea of the cliffhanger: will the alcoholic survive?

This piece was written for "Vertigo On the Ledge," a column that features Vertigo creators.

The Herring Wonder

In 1970, when I was six, I lost my first fight. I was playing by the pond behind my home. I had my sweater pulled over my head so that I would resemble Spider-Man. I was alone, narrating internally my various heroic deeds. Then someone snuck up from behind and pushed me down with quite a bit of savage force.

I figured it was my older sister, and staring through my sweater, I saw that she was fleeing. I chased after her, pulling my sweater down so that I could see better, and then I realized it was not my sister but some older boy, at least nine. I hesitated. Then I remembered I was Spider-Man and kept up my pursuit.

He stopped running and faced me. I brazenly pushed him. Next thing I knew he was sitting on my chest. He reeked horribly of peanut butter, and he pounded my face until I began to bleed. He leaped off and ran away. I staggered up to my house, wailing.

My mother heard my cries and came to me. "Your sweater from Israel!" she shouted. She thought the blood all over me was mud from the pond. I could hardly articulate what had happened, but she quickly caught on and held me in her arms. I had to be taken to a doctor—my nose was fractured and wouldn't stop bleeding. A vein inside my nose had to be cauterized.

In 1974, in the fourth grade, I had my next loss. Two boys, after school, called me and my friend "dirty Jews." We chased after them, which was insane. They were the class bullies and must have run simply to lure us into the woods by the school.

In the sylvan shadows, we paired off. I began with the lesser bully and was soon sitting triumphantly on his chest, but then looked over at my friend and he was in the exact opposite position and was getting choked. So I jumped off the omega bully and tackled the alpha bully. Then the alpha bully was on my chest and down came the fist and there went my nose again.

After that I retired for ten years, until 1984, when I was twenty and living in Paris. At the time, I was very much under the influence of the short stories of Hemingway, and, subsequently, I got into a bar-brawl with a Frenchman, whose father was probably a leader in the resistance. The fight was over a girl. I had picked up a Danish model and he tried to take her away from me and so I had pushed him. This Gallic champion then broke my nose, split my lip, and kneed me in the side of the head.

This precipitated another retirement from fighting, which lasted twelve years. Then in 1996, while living in New York, I called a gay phone-sex line. It only cost fifteen cents a minute. The straight line cost $3.99 a minute. Being broke was affecting my sexuality. On the phone line, I met a man who wanted to box in a hotel room. We met up and I thoroughly routed him. Well, I landed one punch and he jabbed his hip into a dresser and had to stop. But my record, as a fighter, was now 1–3. At last there was something to show in the victory column. Granted, it wasn't the most noble of victories, but you take what you can get.

Three years later, in 1999, I recounted this tale of my hotel-room triumph on the stage of a nightclub, Fez, which was on Lafayette Street in the East Village. A performance artist in the audience, a friend of mine named David Leslie, took offense at my story since he had once fought, in 1988, the future heavyweight champ Riddick Bowe on a crossing of the Staten Island Ferry. It was a performance piece, a kind of Evel Knievel–meets–George Plimpton stunt, and so Leslie wanted to be considered the only artist-boxer in the East Village. Thus, shortly after hearing my story at Fez, he

challenged me to a boxing match, which I accepted, and I immediately dubbed myself "the Herring Wonder." I don't know why
this name came to me, but it did.

I saw myself as a reincarnation of an early-twentieth-century
Jewish boxer, who would train by eating herring. But in addition
to consuming that omega-3-rich fish, I also worked out for two
months at Gleason's in Brooklyn, the world's most famous boxing
gym. Our fight was to be held November 10 at Angel Orensanz,
the nineteenth-century synagogue that had been converted into a
performance venue.

A week before the fight, while sparring with a training partner,
my nose, once again, was broken. The pain was devastating and
my face swelled up. By the next day, I had two black eyes from
blood running off from my fractured nose bone. Leslie, nevertheless, convinced me to go through with the fight. He was producing the whole thing and had sold six hundred tickets. He said he
wouldn't go for my head. A professional boxer would never fight
with a broken nose, but I was a writer, so what the hell, and, too,
my friend promised that he wouldn't go for my head (i.e., my
nose).

On November 10, I entered the ring in that old synagogue,
carrying a jar of herring, and my fans in the crowd waved silver herrings made from cardboard and aluminum. My entrance
music was supposed to be "Hava Nagila," but the CD player
jammed.

In the first round of our four-round fight, Leslie, whose fight
name was "the Impact Addict," pinned my arm and struck me in
the head nine times. Our agreement before the fight had obvi-
ously been forgotten, which was for the best—the crowd got their
money's worth and they went nuts.

In the second round, Leslie rebroke my nose. After the four
rounds were over, I had a concussion and whiplash, my jaw was
knocked out of line, and my ribs were bruised. I had been naive
to enter the ring with a busted nose. A fight is a fight. Anything
can happen. I did land a few good punches, but overall, it was a

hellish experience, made worse by the feeling that my friend had betrayed me.

Traumatized by the match, which, naturally, I lost (my record was now 1–4), I ended up a few weeks later in Havana, Cuba, on something of a bender. One afternoon, tipsy and despairing, I was coming up the stairs of the Hotel Nacional. A young man in a straw hat stopped me.

"Are you Jonathan Ames, the fighter, the Herring Wonder?" he asked.

I pulled myself erect. I was an internationally recognized pugilist!

"Yes, I am," I said.

"I saw your fight. You were great! . . . Well, I have to run, catch this tour bus. Good-bye!"

No longer despairing, I swaggered into the lobby of the hotel and bellied up to the bar. I was a fighter on vacation in Havana, Cuba! I was still a loser, but for once I felt like a winner.

EPILOGUE

Shortly after writing this piece, completely certain that my life as a boxer was over, I was challenged by Soho Press to fight a Canadian writer, Craig Davidson. Davidson has written a novel called *The Fighter* and promoted it in Canada last year by fighting a poet. Now the book is coming out in the States and Soho Press must have gotten wind of my exploits as the Herring Wonder and challenged me on behalf of Davidson.

Perhaps because I am somewhat insane, I accepted this throwing-down of the glove, as it were, and I am, once again, coming out of retirement. I am forty-three years old.

I have commenced training at Gleason's and will face Davidson, who is thirty-one, on July 26, 2007. Our bout will be a part of a night of amateur fights being held outdoors on Pier 84 in Manhattan. The evening is being called "Rumble by the River."

I don't know what will become of me. One thing is nearly certain—if history has taught me anything—my poor nose will bear the brunt of my folly.

So in advance, like a character out of Gogol, I offer this apology to my poor, misshapen, wounded beak: *I am sorry that you will be hurt.*

EPILOGUE II

About six months have passed since my fight with Craig Davidson, whose fight moniker was and is "the Crippler."

Before I describe this brutal fight, let me backtrack a little. First of all, I was disqualified from the Rumble by the River for being too old. It was to be a night of sanctioned amateur bouts, and opponents were not to be separated by more than ten years, for insurance reasons. At the time of the fight, I was twelve years older than the Crippler. We learned of my disqualification two weeks before our bout and it was a tough blow. It was the notion of fighting by the river which had drawn me out of retirement in the first place. When Soho Press challenged me, they had cleverly sent a photo of what the ring looked like by the Hudson as the sun set—a picture taken at the 2006 edition of Rumble by the River. And this had been too romantic an opportunity to pass up—a boxing match by the river with at least a thousand people in attendance!

But it was not meant to be, so we quickly rejiggered the event and it was rescheduled for Tuesday, July 26, at Gleason's. This would give me a home-court advantage, but there was nowhere else really to hold the fight.

Leading up to the match, my training had gone fairly well, though it was far from easy. Eight years before, in preparation for my fight against the Impact Addict, I had trained five days a week. But now, at the age of forty-three, I could only train for about three or four days. I was experiencing severe and excruciating tendinitis in my biceps and elbows, and needed to ice my arms for about an hour after working out.

My schedule was, roughly, Monday, Wednesday, Friday, and Saturday, and each day I would work out for about two hours. My trainer, Grant Seligson, had me hitting the bag quite a lot and we also did a lot of defensive drills. I had two training partners, Bill Nemes and my old opponent, David Leslie, who came out of his own retirement from the ring to work with me. We called our small group "Camp Herring." David and I had patched our friendship back together over the years, and to have him in my camp was an interesting turnabout. It was kind of like Rocky working with Apollo Creed in one of the *Rocky* films, though I'm not sure which one it was, perhaps it was *Rocky III*.

Every member of Camp Herring had a nickname. I was, naturally, "Herring." David, because he complained a lot, despite being tough, was called "Princess D" or just "Princess" for short. Grant, being our leader, was called "General Grant," and Bill was "Captain Semen" because he looks like a sea captain with a thick brown beard and his last name, Nemes, when spelled backward is, conveniently, "semen."

My biggest concern in preparing for the fight was to not get my nose broken again. The solution Camp Herring came up with was for me to wear Princess D's ancient headgear from when he fought Riddick Bowe in 1988. It was a hard piece of leather, shaped like a baseball catcher's mask, and it had a bar down the middle for protecting one's nose. Visibility wasn't great and the thing was quite uncomfortable, but unless that bar was broken my nose would be safe. There was a problem, though. Because the leather was so old and hardened, when I got hit it was like a double blow—my sparring partner's gloved hand and then the mask. Also, because of the bar down the middle, which was connected to the chin-piece, the shock of the blows to my head was distributed in an odd way, such that a lot of the force was going to my jaw.

Well, starting about five weeks before the fight, my jaw kept getting knocked out of line. One's jaw is sort of like a typewriter—

it slides back and forth. A day or two after sparring, my jaw would come back into line, but two weeks before the fight, my jaw was, seemingly, permanently out of line and I couldn't get it to fall back in place. It was very sore, I couldn't bite down, and I was getting freaked out. I had a brutal three-round spar with a twenty-five-year-old boxer (the whole gym gathered as we pummeled each other) and afterward my jaw was really a mess. I told an old trainer at the gym what was going on and he told me that I needed to wear regular headgear that wouldn't send all the reverberations into my jawbone. I explained to him that my nose was so big that regular headgear didn't protect it, and he said, "Well, I'd rather have a broken nose than a broken jaw and drink my meals through a straw for six weeks."

This was not what I wanted to hear, but there was nothing to be done. I decided to stick with the old headgear, rather than make a change at the last moment. The day of the fight, I had a late morning meeting in midtown with an executive at HBO. I thought of canceling the meeting, but it's not easy to tell someone at HBO that you have a boxing match and could you reschedule? And as a somewhat starving writer, if someone from HBO wants to meet you, you had better not make it too hard for them.

So on my way to midtown, I stopped at Paragon Sports near Union Square, hoping to find a better mouth-guard, the piece of plastic you bite down on to protect your teeth. I thought that perhaps a more sophisticated guard could help my jaw from getting broken against the Crippler. I had been using an old-fashioned "boil and bite" guard—you boil a semicircle piece of plastic and then pop it in your mouth and it conforms to your teeth. But I had heard that there were fancier guards, thus the trip to Paragon.

Sure enough, in the boxing section of the store there were plenty of mouth-guards, and with one of them came a diagram of the human skull with the brain and jawbone visible inside the boundaries of the skull. It was drawn in profile, and the brain, from this angle, looked like the state of Florida, and the diagram showed that the back of the jawbone was right next to the lower tip of the brain, the Florida Panhandle, if you will. This was very disturbing. Next to the diagram was a written explanation that when the jawbone is hit in the corner, right by the hinge, the bone comes in contact with the brain, causing knockouts and even death, which was why it was important to wear a good mouth-guard.

I nearly vomited.

I'm a squeamish person.

I didn't like to see a soft-looking brain, which could easily pass for my brain, right next to a hard-looking jawbone. And as it was, I was already having all sorts of jaw paranoia and pain.

I didn't buy the mouth-guard. I didn't want the diagram anywhere near me and I fled Paragon and went to HBO. I didn't do very well in the meeting. The whole time I was thinking about the insanity of getting back into the ring and that the Crippler was going to bang my jaw, which, already tenderized and out of line, was then going to hit the lower tip of my brain and I was going to die. I was going to die to help another writer promote his book. What the hell was I doing? If I was going to put my life at risk, I should at least be doing something truly heroic and decent, like chaining myself to a tree for Greenpeace or reporting from Baghdad.

So I went home from HBO and took to my bed. My girlfriend showed up and we lay there and I told her that I was very upset about my jaw. We did a meditation that she had learned and it seemed to help. Then we took the subway to Gleason's. We were both wearing these very attractive Camp Herring T-shirts that Princess D had designed, replete with a silver herring on the front.

We arrived at the gym around 6:45 and I started to warm up. The Crippler showed up and we shook hands. I bore him no ill will. We had met briefly a few weeks before and he seemed like a good, sweet kid. His parents came down with him from Canada to cheer him on and I met them as well. After my quick handshakes with the Crippler family, we went to different parts of the gym. I moved around one of the spare rings, shadowboxing, and the place began to fill up. In total, about three hundred people turned out,

and my favorite bookstore, BookCourt, was there to sell books. All
the regular fighters in the gym kept on training.

Around 8:15, to get things off to a good start, my friend the
hula-hoop artist, Miss Saturn, performed to "Relax" by Frankie
Goes to Hollywood, swirling her hoops to the music and the
crowd's enthusiastic applause.

Then our announcer, the lit-blogger Edward Champion, looking resplendent in a rented tuxedo, stepped through the ropes
and called the Crippler into the ring. Crippler was in great, fierce
shape—he had been training five days a week and he looked enormous, especially his arms. He's about six-two and he looked to
weigh about 175 pounds. He had three to four inches on me and
about eighteen pounds, plus the twelve years. I'm five-ten and for
the fight I was my usual weight of about 157.

When Edward Champion called me into the ring, my "fans"
went nuts. They waved silver herrings, once again made from foil
and cardboard, and they screamed lustily, chanting, "Herring!
Herring! Herring!"

An added bonus for me was that a contingent of about ten
workers from the Jewish smoked-fish store, Russ and Daughters,
had shown up. They had gotten wind of the fight and were spon-
soring the after-party. They were all wearing T-shirts that said
on the back "Herring et Veritas," which is a departure from their
usual slogan—"Lox et Veritas."

After my introduction, Edward Champion called for our card
"girls"—Harry "the Mangina" Chandler and Valmonte Sprout, my
dear friends whom I call Mangie and Sproutie. Sproutie had her
whole body painted red and she was topless. Mangie had on a
flesh-colored rubber cap he had made and the tip of the cap was
painted to look like a nipple, turning his head into a breast. He was
also wearing a pale full-body stocking with his mangina sticking
out of an opening in the necessary location. His fake leg looked
jaunty coming out of the body stocking, and he put Sproutie on
his shoulders and carried her about the ring, while she held up a
card with a glittering roman numeral one.

Then the happy couple (they've been together for several years) got out of the ring and the bell was struck and the fight began. I wanted to feel the Crippler out, not go on the attack immediately, so I moved to my right and he came toward me . . . He started to make a move, cocking back his right fist, and I immediately threw a left jab right into his face, followed by a quick right-hand. Both blows nailed him quite well and he fell into my arms, clinching me. (That's me on the right, throwing a right.)

This was something that would happen throughout the fight—he would lose balance and fall into me and we'd hold on to each other. I didn't mind this at all—by holding on to him, like a dance partner, I could shave seconds off the clock, seconds that weren't too draining. The main thing with boxing is that it's the most fatiguing sport in the world. I don't know what it is, but the constant movement, the carrying of the fourteen-ounce gloves, the fear of this person across from you trying to hurt you, the pain of the blows, the force it requires to throw punches—well, it's all wildly, wildly exhausting. Thus, I didn't mind the clinches one bit, and in the first round, he also stumbled so badly that he knocked both of us to the ground, which, again, I didn't mind. I took precious, long seconds to get up.

When I wasn't trying to use up the clock that first round, I did hit him quite a lot. He kept trying to unload these haymaker right-hands, which were easy to see coming, and so I was able to block them or slip them and then would counter with left jabs, straight right-hands, and left hooks. When the bell rang, I was tired, but feeling good, and retreated to my corner, where Grant poured some water into my mouth and told me I was doing great. (That's me on the left, landing a left.)

Mangie and Sproutie forgot to come in the ring before the second round, which was comedically typical of them, so when they entered the ring before the third round, they chased each other about, Mangie carrying the round-two card and Sproutie carrying the round-three card.

Anyway, back to the fight story: In the second round, the Crippler nailed me with a good body blow, but I had so much adrenaline going that I didn't really feel it. Another time, it was either the second or third round, he got me up against the ropes and threw about five right-hands into the left side of my rib cage, but, again, because of adrenaline, the blows didn't really hurt.

One time, I think it was in the second round, we were in a clinch and the ref came over and said, as he did throughout the fight, "Break, break," and I pretended not to hear him, giving myself more seconds of rest, and then the ref said, *"Break!"* and I said, "What?" like I didn't understand him, giving me a few more seconds . . .

During all three rounds, I kept nailing the Crippler. One time, I hit him quite hard with a left hook and I saw his eyes go glassy and I said, "Are you okay?" This wasn't very rugged of me, but the words slipped out. During my Camp Herring spars I would often say "Sorry!" when I hit someone hard, and Princess D and Captain Semen and General Grant would all yell at me: *"Don't say you're sorry!"*

Luckily, the Crippler never was able to land a blow to my head—it was a miracle. My messed-up jaw didn't get any more messed up. He tried, repeatedly, to hit me in the head, but all the defensive skills I had learned from General Grant had paid off. Then, mercifully, the bell rang at the end of the third round (it was a typical amateur-length bout—three two-minute rounds—whereas my mad battle against the Impact Addict was four three-minute rounds) and it was over! I had survived and I had won. My record had improved to 2–4! I was incredibly elated. My nose was in one piece and my jaw hadn't been further damaged (it took about a month, but eventually my jaw did fall back into place). I took off my headgear and my girlfriend climbed up on the lip of the ring, and leaning over the ropes, I kissed her. It was like we were in our own old-time Hollywood boxing movie! It was the best kiss of my life.

Because it was a nonsanctioned amateur bout, the Crippler and I were both given trophies, and the Crippler, being the good guy that he is, said into the microphone, which had been handed to him by Edward Champion, that it had been a tough fight, but that I had won fair and square. When the microphone came to me, I told the audience to buy the Crippler's book and then I gave a long and loud "hairy call," this sound I've been making since childhood, which sonically resembles the blowing of the shofar, which is only fitting for a boxer known as "the Herring Wonder."

The first part of this essay and the first epilogue were published in the online edition of McSweeney's *in 2007. To read Craig Davidson's account of the fight, go to www.penguinblogs.ca/davidson/archives/00000167.html.*

And to see more pictures of the fight, go to www.gawker.com and search for "Jonathan Ames and Craig Davidson."

SHORT STORIES

Book Tour Diary

At the hotel. Leaving for the airport in a little while. A successful reading last night. A lot of people. Sold a lot of books.

Made out with S. in the stacks, but she had to go to her boyfriend. One of the people from the bookstore saw us, must think I'm a nut.

"I want you to pull my hair and I want to give you a blow job in the car and have you come in my mouth," she said.

But I was the prude. Didn't want to do it in her car, and, also, I felt that she would regret it immediately afterward. How could she go to her boyfriend with the taste of my semen in her mouth? I thought she would feel bad and I didn't want to do that to her. Also, I never like to come in someone's mouth. As soon as I'm coming I think that it must taste terrible and so I derail my own orgasm.

But I was disappointed that she couldn't be with me. Wanted to experience her again. A year ago, it was carnal, depraved sex when I came out here for the hardcover. I love her smell. Whatever it is she puts on her skin. She put my hand to her throat in the stacks. She likes to be choked, slapped, taken violently. Says her boyfriend won't do that stuff. But I did it for her. I wanted to please her.

So after kissing her last night I was all riled up. I went on craigslist and there was this beautiful tranny. I couldn't resist. I called her and she said her name was Savannah, but I think that's just her craigslist name. She must have her real boy name, her real girl name, and then her working-girl name. A lot of names.

Took a taxi to her around one a.m. Rough part of town. Literally, across a river and some train tracks. She lives in a boarding-house, like something out of a Jim Thompson novel. New York doesn't have things like that anymore, places where you can live and not spend too much money. The walls of her room were covered with hundreds of cutouts of models and actresses. Her bed had a canopy she built, with gauze all around it. It was like a serial killer's apartment, this temple of femininity. She was eerily beautiful. Miniskirt, tall and blonde, a perfectly feminine face, gorgeous smooth legs, lovely mouth. How does this happen?

I gave her a hundred and fifty bucks and we kissed, standing there. I held her close. She tasted good.

She pulled me down on to the bed for more kissing. Her blouse came off. She had these pubescent-size breasts from female hormones. They were beautiful. I kissed them gently. She smelled nicely of perfume. I'm a sucker for perfume. Then she got a condom, lube, positioned herself doggy-style, lifted the skirt, guided me into her. I had been there all of ten minutes. Never saw her cock, like *M. Butterfly*. Her heels stayed on, which I liked. I held those small breasts, and then she lowered herself to the bed, her stomach flat against it, and I kissed her neck, and I had that fleeting illusion of being in love.

And then she came—I guess from rubbing herself against the bed. She screamed out "I'm coming," and so that made me come. It wasn't as good as a real girl but the transgression of it was thrilling, though as soon as it was over, the despair was immediate and swift. I felt panicked and dirty. What had I done? Why couldn't I have just stayed in the hotel?

Her sink was low, came to my waist, and I washed myself in it. My cock looked like this pathetic pink instrument in that sink, her makeup all around the edge of the porcelain. There was a razor for her legs and I thought of cutting off my cock, and how I'd have to saw at myself with that little razor. It was a flash of thought-violence. Then I almost laughed, a strange macabre laugh, thinking about my cock in her sink, left there like some horrible, grotesque sacrifice.

But the washing-up did help. What we had done wasn't so terrible, and I didn't flee. She wanted me to stay for a little bit. So we sat and talked. She put on a robe and looked demure. She's only twenty. She thought I was thirty-five and complimented me for looking so young at forty-one, which was nice of her. She told me about taking hormones. I said, "Be careful about your liver." "Why?" she asked, a flicker of concern in her eyes, of self-preservation, which I was glad to see. I told her that I heard the hormones can hurt your liver, that she should look into it. I told her I read about it in the science section of the *Times,* this article on transsexuals. But this didn't impress her. She needs to know what she's taking, be aware of the side effects.

We talked some more and she told me she was always different, playing with Barbies. Never met her biological father. Said she was a miracle baby, that her mother's tubes had been tied and burnt. She said burnt. Yet somehow the mother got pregnant. I asked her if she was going to get a sex change. "I don't know, not if I can't get off," she said. I thought about how she came from having me in her. She was supernaturally beautiful. An American changeling. She got the wrong hormones in her mother's womb. Came out a boy, but her brain told her otherwise. She kissed me good-bye. She said, "You're sweet."

Will stop now. Have to get cab to the airport.

APRIL 12

4:30 P.M.

A few hours later. In ——. I'm on a bench, in a park, on a cliff, overlooking the bay, sailboats in the distance.

The cabbie from the airport said, "I used to believe in good luck, but now I believe in bad luck since it's the only kind I have." He said he was an actor and once he got out of debt, he said he planned to go to L.A. He was in his late forties, fading looks, blond hair, a receding chin. He had been handsome once but there was something off about him. Drugs or alcohol or bipolar. Something. I gave him a big tip. He was all obsequious after the tip, taking my bag into the hotel for me, fawning over me. He asked what I was doing in town, and I told him I was a writer, that my paperback had come out, and he gave me his last card, which was a little dirty, and it said "actor" under his name.

APRIL 13
3:00 A.M.

Another good reading. Just got back. Read with D., who's kind of a local celebrity, so there was a huge crowd. Afterward, D. had a party at a bar, a lot of people. I was drawn to this sexy, buxom girl named T., but her friend, M., was all over me, asking me to dance, pressing against me. She was a little drunk and while I was dancing with her, T. left. Then M. asked me to go home with her. She's twenty-four, a little nutty, a grad student in art history. Beautiful eyes. Sweet little breasts. We took a taxi. She said, "I don't usually do this." "Do what?" I asked. "Take home older, strange writers." "I should hope not," I said. I was feeling witty, almost happy.

I went down on her and she came and it was nice. Then she didn't have a condom, but she found one in her roommate's room, which was good luck, and the roommate was out. The sex was okay. More about her later—what she said about her mother, who has cancer, which was very heartbreaking.

APRIL 15
1:20 P.M.

So I had an amazing time in —— on the fourteenth. Sold forty books. Was signing books and these three Asian girls gave me candy and a card and a little stuffed animal. They were giggling. It was very sweet. And then this gorgeous raven-haired girl gives me a note after I signed her book. She had this somewhat unusual, beautiful upturned nose. And she had green eyes and very pale skin in contrast with her long, dark hair. She was about five-four, not too tall, but statuesque—full breasts and ass. Was wearing this sleeveless white top and tight jeans. She had beautiful arms. I love women's arms, and I love the armpit. For some reason, as I've gotten older, I've become obsessed with licking a woman's armpit, this hidden secret place, like it's another pussy or something. I must be losing my mind.

Anyway, I didn't get a chance to read the girl's note, just put it in my pocket; there were other people waiting on line, and it would look weird reading some note from a beautiful girl. But then someone from the bookstore brings me another note, it's from the same girl, it says, "I'm the girl with the dark hair who gave you the note. I'm serious. Call me."

And I look at the first note and there's a number. So after I sign everybody's book, I call her. She picks me up outside the bookstore and there's another girl in the car. A blonde, a little harder-looking, kind of a cheap look, but also attractive. They both have the same first name, L., which is strange and they agreed that it was strange but it was part of what drew them to each other. L. #1, who gave me the note, runs a catering company, and L. #2 is a buyer or something for a department store.

We go to a bar and they tell me their story. They're both twenty-nine and they're married and they're secret lesbian lovers and their husbands don't know. The men just think that their wives have these girls' nights out. They get cheap hotel rooms for two or three hours. They also meet up in the afternoon sometimes, when the husbands are at work, and they don't have to pay for a room. But they tell me that L. #2, the blonde, doesn't like to have her pussy licked because when she was fifteen her first boyfriend went down there and came right back up with a disgusted look on his face and said, "I don't like that . . ."

Also, she said she has three brothers and when she was growing up they would call it "Sunday sushi," which struck me as sophisticated—how did her suburban brothers know that sushi was bad on Sundays? Anyway, somehow these two things have made her incapable of letting anyone, including L. #1, go down on her.

So what do they do? I asked. She said that she does it to L. #1. I said, "Well, you see then that it's nice, you should let her do it to you." "I know, that's what I say," said L. #1, but L. #2 said, "I just can't. I have a phobia."

I couldn't believe they were sitting across from me, telling me all this, but L. #1 said that my books made her feel like she could tell me anything. L. #2 hasn't actually read me, but liked the reading.

After all this talk about eating pussy, they announced that even though they had brought me out and were telling me all this stuff, they wanted to make it clear that they couldn't have sex with me. Sex with a man was a level of cheating that was too much for them. I suggested a compromise: that we have a three-way cuddle in my hotel room, and they thought that was queer, but were intrigued.

But L. #2 backed out, said she had to be at work early, so she left and L. #1 came back with me. We had a drink at the hotel bar and then she went up to my room first, by herself. I gave her my key. She said people know her in this town, that there might be a business associate of her husband at the bar, so it would be better if it seemed like she had a drink with me and then left. Her husband knew she was a fan of mine and that she had come to my reading, so it was perfectly legit for her to be at the hotel with me, but she couldn't be seen leaving the bar in my company.

So she slipped out to the elevator, like something out of a fifties movie. It was all very noir. I waited five minutes, as she had instructed, and went up to my room, where she was waiting for me topless. And she had the most amazing body. The most beautiful breasts with gigantic, dark brown nipples. She was half Brazilian, half Irish. "Our pants have to stay on," she said.

We went by the window, looking out over the whole city; we

were on the twenty-eighth floor, the city looked spectacular, all that American money, and I held her from behind, cupping her breasts in my hand, weighing them.

Then we got on the bed and made out—making out was acceptable to her—and I nursed on her breasts and I came in my pants rubbing against the bed. She could tell I came and she laughed. It was actually quite heavenly. I said, as we hugged good-bye at my door, "Was this okay? I hope you don't feel bad."

"I don't feel bad. Maybe tomorrow I'll feel bad, but not right now. This is something I wanted to do for a while, ever since I first read you. I was worried I wouldn't like you in person. You're quieter than I thought you'd be, but you're sweet."

She and Savannah think I'm sweet. I don't know if they're right or wrong. After she left, I lay on the bed and marveled in my mind at her beauty, and I felt a kind of giddy gratitude for my crazy sex life.

APRIL 17

11:30 A.M.

Plane again. Flying home. —— was quiet. A smaller crowd but nice people. I went back to the hotel right after the reading and behaved myself. Then in ——, the next day, things were completely nuts.

K. met me at the airport. She had been e-mailing me for months and wanted to meet me at the airport to welcome me to her city. I said that she didn't have to meet me, that the publisher often had someone there, but she kept on insisting, telling me it was her fantasy, and that from the airport she wanted to come with me straight to my hotel if we felt okay in each other's presence.

I gave in to her and she met me, holding a card with my name and smiling really big. She was tiny, maybe five-one, and she was dressed like an adolescent, though she's thirty-three and married. She had a child's backpack on with these little Japanese buttons all over it, a pink jacket, jeans with yellow patches on the knees, and little purple sneakers. Her face was pretty (just like her pictures in the e-mails), but her tininess and the child clothing made me feel funny. We got a cab. We sat in the backseat, quiet and awkward. I didn't know if I could do it. It was too strange. But she was looking at me with such adoration, so I took her hand and as soon as we held hands and she squeezed my hand with happiness, I knew I could make love to her.

We went right to my room. I asked about her husband. She told me in her e-mails that they have an open marriage, but I still felt worried about it. So many of the women I'm meeting have a boyfriend or are married. It's like a weird run in cards.

I said to K., "Are you sure he doesn't mind?"

"He doesn't mind," she said. "All he said was 'I just don't want to hear about dick size.'"

This made me like her husband a lot, like he was some kind of brother or something.

Well, after that, right away we were in bed and I was glad the clothing had come off. She was tiny but it was the body of a woman. She didn't want me to go down on her. She just wanted me in her immediately. I put on a condom and it was a brutal, fast lay. I appreciated the animalness of it—that we had met at the airport forty-five minutes before and then we were in bed copulating.

We lay there, her head on my chest, like we were old-time lovers, and I tried to get at why she wanted to do it with me so bad, and she said, "To get the power back. When I like an artist, it's like they have power over me, but by sleeping with you I get the power back and then I also take some of your power. So now I'm even stronger."

She said she had slept with a number of local musicians that she would get infatuated with and a few famous ones, too. She was very matter-of-fact about it all. Even said that I was a notch on her belt.

But what do I get out of all this? I've always been touristic when it comes to sex—a new face, a new body—but mostly, I think, it's affection by committee. I'm incapable of a relationship, but I do want some tenderness, some love. Enough to get by on. I also like to please people. Hard for me to say no. I guess that's my way of being loving.

Anyway, after the reading, K. had a party for me at her house. Her husband was incredibly nice—black-gray hair, good-looking, a little bit older than me, a rugged face, though a bit fey. All their friends were smoking pot from a bong that was this long, green tube coming out of a plastic turtle, but I didn't smoke. Didn't feel like it. The house was filled with odd knickknacks and weird art. I liked the whole scene. Some wonderful nerdy boy with bright red hair was talking to this girl and me about his love of Sam Peckinpah and Bob Dylan. The girl had an enormous nose and big glasses. She was only nineteen and gorgeous in a brainy, secret-sexy way.

Then K. wanted to leave, go back to the hotel with me, and do it again. Her friends didn't know. They thought she was just escorting me home, being an extra-gracious hostess to the visiting writer. She called a taxi and it got there fast and honked. As we left, her husband gave me this gentle kick in the ass and it was the most amazing thing. I turned and looked at him and there was this part benevolent, part mischievous, and tiny part wounded look in his eye. It was like he was the father of some young girl I was dating and he was kicking me in the ass as I headed out the door on a date with his daughter, letting me know that he knew what I would do, but man-to-man he was okay with it, even got a kick out of it, so to speak, though on some level, maybe the truest level, it did pain him. It is definitely one of the oddest moments of my life.

Then their dog slipped out as we were leaving, and she went chasing after it, and I got in the cab so it wouldn't leave, and I was laughing to myself, thinking about that kick, how strange and tender and human it was, and the taxi driver, who was Indian and polite, said, "What are you laughing about, sir?" and I said, "Life," and he smiled in the rearview mirror. Then she got the dog back inside, and from the front door she called out to her husband, "I love you." We got back to the hotel and it was another brutal quick one and she seemed very satisfied.

She called me this morning and said that she and her husband stayed up till six talking about everything. She told him that I was rough in bed. I said, "Was that all right?"

"Oh, yeah," she said. "I've never had it so rough but I loved it." I was surprised to hear this, I didn't think I had been too rough, and I thought of all the musicians she had slept with—weren't any of them rough?

Then she said that her husband liked hearing about the roughness. According to her, he had said, with admiration, "Who knew that under such a quiet demeanor he would be like that."

I sort of feel like I love them. I should move in with them. They could put me in some room, like an animal, and just take care of me. I'd give them all my money. They could own me.

Well, the book tour is over. Nobody would believe the life I lead. I don't believe it. I feel embarrassed doing what I do. But I guess I give some people pleasure with my books. Like a clown. It's my only justification. Plane is going to land soon. We're hitting some turbulence and I feel frightened. I don't want to die in a plane. I don't want to die at all.

Ping (the magazine of the Henry Miller Library), 2008

A Walk Home

The night of the attack, I parked my car, as was my habit, near the canal. The Gowanus Canal. In that area, the streets are desolate and perhaps a little dangerous so there's plenty of parking, and I used to put the car over there so I wouldn't have to get up early in the morning to move it.

I work from home and prefer to sleep late. But on my Brooklyn street, you have to wake up at 8:20 a.m. so as to move the car by 8:30. Also, you have to move the car again at 9:40 (after double-parking it at 8:30) . . . Anyway, I'm getting into the boring rules of New York City parking—I apologize. The point is, I like to sleep until ten or eleven and so I would park my ten-year-old Ford Taurus station wagon near the Gowanus, where I could just leave the car and not worry about moving it in the morning.

So the night in question I parked the car and it was around three o'clock. It was very cold out, a real February night, and whenever I was over there, like that night, I would try to come up with some pun in my mind about the Gowanus Canal, because the word 'anus' is in Gowanus and the word 'anal' is in Canal, and because the Gowanus smells. Even on a cold night. But I never came up with a good pun. The best I could do was to pronounce both words with a long *a*: Gow-AY-nus C-AY-nal.

I probably couldn't come up with a good pun because the canal doesn't smell like an anus. Anuses, I have found, don't smell too bad. When I lick a girl from behind, my nose is in her ass or near her ass and there's usually this fruity smell, which must come from the decomposition of sugar. I used to lick girls' asses, but then I learned that you can give girls urinary tract infections going from their ass to their pussy, so I stopped doing that for the most part.

Anyway, I'm on a ridiculous tangent . . . so I was walking up Bond Street by the Gowanus housing projects, about six blocks from where I live on the gentrified streets. I was walking on the street itself, to give myself the most space to move should there be a mugging—on the sidewalk you can be too easily pinned if your attackers hide behind a car and then jump out at you. Ideally, from the mugger's point of view, one would be in front of you and one behind you—then you're trapped.

Yet most of the muggings in the neighborhood—and there have been dozens—don't seem to employ this method. According to my friends who have been assaulted, the muggers, brandishing knives, never guns, just come at the victim from the front, which could allow a person to turn around and run, but it's probably scary to turn your back on muggers.

But my girlfriend—now ex—did just that three years ago. She was confronted by three teenage boys and she refused to give them her money and she turned and ran. But they caught her, spun her around, threw her down, and took a little over a hundred dollars from her. Thank God that's all they did. But she was terribly distraught and frightened and hysterical. I don't think it led to our breakup, but maybe it didn't help.

It was irrational on her part, but she thought I should have been there, protected her. It became symbolic of my other failures to protect her, and I haven't really loved anybody since. Well, maybe I have, but I don't let it get too far. It's too scary to be close to someone—their dreams for their life become so palpable and their innocent beauty in wanting just their little bit of happiness is too much for me. I don't want to bear witness to their disappointment. But this isn't very respectful of me. I should have more faith in their strength.

So that night I was four blocks from my street, from relative safety, when two black teenagers stepped out from the front of a van. The van had given them cover and they were about ten yards—two parked cars—from me. There was plenty of bilious light coming off the streetlamps, but there was no one around. It was too cold out and too late for there to be people walking about, and there weren't even any cars, no one driving anywhere at three a.m. in this part of town. To my left were the vast buildings of the prisonlike projects and to my right were the empty warehouse streets of the canal area.

They walked toward me. I squeezed the tip of my baton, which was in the palm of my right hand. The shaft—the rest of the twelve-inch, black-painted steel baton—was hidden up the sleeve of my winter coat. I quickly looked to my right and my left and behind me—there were no others. I started angling to my left, crossing the road so as to avoid them and give them a chance not to do this, but they sidled to their right, staying less than paral- lel with me as they narrowed the distance between us to about fifteen feet—one car length. I thought of sprinting to my right, passing them like a football player returning a punt—they'd have to backpedal for a moment and turn, which could give me enough time. I also thought of doing what my girlfriend did—fleeing the other way.

But I did neither. I kept moving forward, not running. They were young and tall and wearing sneakers. I'm forty-two and was wearing leather-soled shoes. I had been at a play and then a very late dinner—I was nicely dressed. I'm still a fast runner, I've stayed lean even as I've aged, but I figured they could catch me. Also, I was not wanting to give in to some kind of racism, or, rather, I didn't want *them* to think I was giving in to racism, that I was another white person judging them unfairly, confirming *their* prejudices— maybe their sidling across the street seemingly to intersect me was just their route and their intention was innocent. I wasn't worried about my own racism—I'm not too bad on that front. I don't think poorly of the blacks that live in the projects. I think poorly of man, of economics, of society, of America.

My one area of weakness—where perhaps my liberalism crumbles—may be my annoyance with the way some black mothers treat their children on the subway, the way they yell at them and threaten them and belittle them and slap them. More than once I've tried to intervene and always I get the same response—that it's none of my business and I should back the fuck off. But I don't blame these few black mothers who behave this way. Like I said, I blame man, economics, society, and America. I did read some article once by a black professor where he wrote about some of the harsh parenting techniques in the black community as still being in place from the era of slavery, that it had been a coping device at that time, a way to harden the children, and this professor's article confirmed what I had seen on the subways and in the playgrounds by the projects—what appears to be unnecessary cruelty. And so this article, since it was written by a black man, made me feel less bad, less guilty, for what I had observed, for noticing it, for thinking what felt like a kind of prejudice and judgment.

Anyway, the intention of the boys was not innocent. I moved back to my right as a sort of final test—a last hope—and they moved with me. Whatever prejudices I had and they had were about to converge. One boy looked to be about sixteen—his face was a chalky brown and chubby, not quite a man's face yet, though he was six feet tall and bulky in a down winter coat. He wore baggy jeans and a black winter hat with "NY" on it. The other boy was maybe twenty, dark, and very tall, about six-four. He wore a thin jacket—he must have been cold—and baggy jeans. He had no hat.

They were about six feet from me, we were back near the cars parked on the right, and the older boy said, "What time is it?" It was some kind of opening rhetorical line because the younger one closed in, was two feet from me, and said, "We're going to take your money, faggot," and he drew a fat hunting knife out of the waist of his jeans. I had seen that knife in the army and navy store a few blocks away on Smith Street, and he pointed it at me, just

inches from my stomach, and the other boy closed in and drew out
the same kind of knife.

I let the baton slip down my sleeve real fast so the handle
came to rest in my palm, and I whipped it at the young chubby
boy's hand that held the knife; the end of the baton extended as it
was designed—a steel flexible tube emerged, like a vicious, thick
antenna, and it cut the boy's wrist to the bone; his hand dipped
down as if on a hinge, partially severed, and he screamed and
crumpled to the ground, somehow still holding the knife, and the
other boy spastically lunged at me with his knife and I stepped to
the right and backhanded the baton across his face, cutting him
open from his ear to his mouth, a grotesque red peeling of his
dark flesh, and then I chopped down on his knife hand, ripping it
open, and the knife dropped, and he fell, screaming, and bleeding
terribly.

I stood for a moment, panicked and frightened, and the boys
knelt in front of me mewling and disfigured—the pain was too
great for them to stand up and run or fight. I could have killed
them with that steel baton, the man who sold it to me at a flea
market two years ago said that "it'll cut meat from a bone," and off
and on I had been practicing moves with it in my apartment—I
had been a fencer at NYU as an undergrad, I knew how to use
such a weapon, and so I had carried it for two years at night after
parking, after my girlfriend had moved out.

So I stood there looking at those boys, dizzy, not in my body;
I wanted to say I was sorry, but no words came, and then a car, at
last, pulled up to the corner and stopped, and I ran. Sprinted. Ran
all the way home, the baton back up my sleeve, hidden. I thought
of calling 911 to get an ambulance for the boys, but was too scared
to make the call, to implicate myself, and I just hoped that whoever was in that car had stopped and called for help. I lay in my bed
all night, my clothes on, not sleeping, reliving it over and over.

In the morning, I washed the blood and my fingerprints off
the baton and took it outside, hidden in the sleeve of my coat, but
not touching my skin, just my shirt, and then I let it slip down

to my hand—I was wearing gloves—and I dropped it in a sewer, pretending to tie my shoes. Then I got my car, frightened, expecting to be killed, looking for the boys, expecting them to be there, bandaged, and with a gang of friends. But they weren't there. They wouldn't have any idea which car was mine, or that I had even parked a car, but I was paranoid and full of fear.

The last few weeks, I keep my eye out for them, but I haven't seen them, and I park only on my street, getting up early with the others on my block. I don't want to hurt anyone else.

The L Magazine, 2006

Old Man, Young Girl

A girl called me up. I hadn't seen her in months. She was in my neighborhood. It was night.

I took her to a restaurant. She was prettier than I remembered. Sleek and dark. Nice legs. Smooth skin.

She had to be up early in the morning so I drove her back to her place.

Her room was cluttered, but not in a bad way—it was full of life. Books. Strange art hanging from the ceiling, a sewing machine, two cats, pretty dresses.

We lay down. I held her from behind. I felt soothed.

"I want to take this dress off," she said. "I've been wearing it all day."

So then I kissed her dark nipples. Her breasts were meager but the nipples took care of me.

I looked up from her nipples and she was smiling. Then I kissed her smooth, cool belly. Then I kissed her pussy through her panties. I like to do that—to have that barrier, at least for a moment, to keep me from the prize.

The panties came off. I licked her. I loved it. I love being in there far away from my life.

But she pulled me up to her and said, "I'm impatient." She said it in a good way and got a condom from a drawer next to her bed. All my clothes came off and the condom went on.

It was dark in her room and I was hoping it wasn't a condom

with spermicide. The last time I had been with her, at least six months before, she had given me a condom with spermicide—it was a spermicidal condom, which makes me think of the words "suicidal" and "homicidal" and, anyway, that condom had scorched me. When I had left her I could hardly walk down the street. It did something anti-Pavlovian to me, made me not want to see her again. That, and the sex had been fumbling and I had felt embarrassed, not virile.

You see, I'm forty-seven and she's twenty-two and that fumbling had humiliated me. But this time it went better. I didn't make her come, but I did the best I could and I think it was all right. After about fifteen minutes, though, I thought I might lose my hard-on—the condom was very tight—and so I came.

Then we lay there and she seemed happy. I figured she needed a man inside her, she just needed it, even if there was no love. Later, I got dressed and found the condom wrapper and I put it in my pocket. Outside, under a streetlight, I saw that it was a normal condom. I felt fine. I drove home. I'll see her again.

There was no love, but I haven't loved anyone in a long time.

Esquire, 2006

*This was originally written on a napkin—*Esquire *had a series in which authors composed stories on napkins. To see the original napkin version, go to www. esquire.com/fiction/napkin-project/ESQ0207OldMan?click=main_sr#.*

I Was in Flowers

About five years ago, I went to see this male prostitute. I'm not gay, but something is wrong with me. Something happened in childhood.

So I saw this guy's ad in the *Village Voice* and called him. All it showed was his muscular torso. But that didn't really matter. I don't care what a man looks like. "I saw your ad," I said on the phone. The rest was pretty easy—price, address, time. He could see me in an hour. If it had been any longer, I probably wouldn't have gone. When you have a self-destructive compulsion, you need to act on it fast.

He lived in a five-story walk-up on a busy avenue—bars, delis, restaurants, banks, and drugstores. He buzzed me through the vestibule. I climbed the dirty, anonymous stairs to the third floor and was so nervous I thought I might faint or have some kind of convulsion. I couldn't stop trembling. He opened the door a crack, saw I was harmless, and let me in.

He was wearing an old blue robe and had a glass of whiskey in his hand. He offered to make me a drink, but I only had a glass of water. He had me sit in this old-fashioned, men's-club armchair and he sat on his bed. It took small-talk about the weather for me to stop shaking.

"What's it like out?" he said. "I haven't been out all day."

"It's a mild night," I said. It was early May, around eleven o'clock at night.

"I love spring," he said. "I need to get out."

His apartment was crowded and dark. The furniture was too big for a narrow studio. It was the kind of stuff that was supposed to look fancy, like some middle-class family's notion of elegance in their living room (with a touch of hysteria or something)—an elaborate mirrored cabinet, gigantic stained-glass lamps, the armchair I was sitting in, and a faux antique mobile bar with lots of bottles. The wallpaper was a dark, boudoir crimson.

The guy also added to the crowded feeling in the place. He was a big lug—about six-four, 230 pounds, large masculine head, blunt American features, about forty-five, and his hair was close-cropped and receding. He looked like a dock worker, but his furniture was definitely a little queer.

He was a nice guy. Sweet. After he finished his whiskey, he gently asked me for the money and said that I should just put it on the desk—a shiny, fake antique thing loaded up with a messy pile of his mail and a large ashtray of change. I put the money down, one hundred and fifty bucks. He didn't want to touch it; like I said, he was sweet, and so you could tell he didn't want to sully things by directly taking the money for what we were going to do.

He asked if I was gay or bi or straight. I told him I was straight, not much experience, and what I wanted. "Take your clothes off," he said.

I did and he opened his robe and he had a gigantic cock. "Can you put a condom on?" I asked.

"No problem," he said.

He stroked himself to get hard. His body was heavier than his picture in the paper, but not by too much. When he was hard, he put a condom on, and he stayed sitting on the edge of his bed.

The thing was twice the size of mine and most women tell me I have a nice one. I don't know if they're lying or if this guy was unnatural. Once the condom was in place, I got on my knees and sucked it. I could just about get the head in my mouth. It was thrilling for about the first minute and then it got dull. I felt a little ridiculous sucking this big rubbery thing.

We got on the bed. He took the condom off and spooned me. I asked him what his other clients were like. He said they were mostly married men. "Nice guys," he said. "A few regulars." We lay there silently. I felt small in his arms. It sort of reminded me of what I was trying to re-create, which made me feel a little sick, but I tried to get into it, to feel queer and all right with being held by a man. I wondered if this was how girls felt in my arms. I'm six foot and bigger than all the girls I see.

"How old are you?" he asked.

"Thirty-two," I said.

"Just a baby," he said.

Then he lubed me up, put on a new condom, bent me over the edge of the bed, and somehow got the thing in there. "Please don't move," I said.

It hurt and then I got used to it, but it never felt good. I thought something might go wrong with my bowels, told him as much, and he pulled out. He washed up, put on his third condom of the night, and I sucked him some more, again kneeling on the floor. I masturbated my cock, which never got hard, but I came on a paper towel he had given me so as not to mess up his rug. He didn't come.

I stood up and he let me rinse off in the shower. His bathroom was small and a little cleaner than my own. He hugged me good-bye and gave me a kiss on the cheek.

"You're good-looking," he said. "Next time you'll be more relaxed. We can enjoy each other more."

I got the hell out of there. I hated myself for about two hours, took a scalding bath back at my place, and then was able to sleep. The next day my ass was sore, but two days later it wasn't and I forgot about the whole thing.

Three years later I called him again.

It was around ten o'clock at night. I'd just had a date with a nice woman that had ended early and I was walking to the subway. Then I felt the insanity hit me. It's a combination of fierce loneliness and self-hate, and you need to do something to yourself right away to make it go away. It's like a mental cicada. I can go months, even years, without it happening, and then it's there.

So I found a *Village Voice*. I took it from one of the ubiquitous, battered red boxes, and it's a good thing they're all over the place, so if you're hit by madness and have to find a prostitute right away to humiliate you, it's not a lot of work. I went to the back pages and spotted his ad. I was pretty sure that it was his torso. There were a couple of other pictures of torsos, but I was sure that I remembered his specific ad.

It was a cold night and under a streetlight I was looking at the *Voice,* waiting for the sidewalk to be empty so nobody would know what I was doing (as if they would know or care, but shame makes you self-centered), and then I called his number on my cell phone.

"I saw your ad," I said.

"Oh, yeah . . . When do you want to see me?"

"Now," I said.

He hesitated, then: "Okay. It's a cold night. I could use some warming up. Have I seen you before?"

"Yes," I said. "A few years ago."

"It's one-fifty. That all right?"

"Yeah, that's fine," I said.

"Well, it's freezing out. Let's make it one hundred."

I didn't know why he was lowering his price. Maybe he thought I wouldn't come. "Okay," I said.

"You remember my address?"

"Tell me again," I said.

I went to an ATM and got out two hundred dollars, then took a cab to his place. I remembered the staircase. I was trembling again. He opened the door a crack and then let me in. He was in the same robe and had a whiskey in his hand, but he had changed. His head was shaved and it didn't look good on him. His head was too large and the baldness made his skull look obscene. He had also put on about thirty pounds—now he definitely didn't resemble his ad. That may have been why he lowered the price.

"Do you remember me?" I asked.

He studied me. He seemed drunk. "I do," he said. "I remember your handsome face. But you never came back . . . Want a drink?"

"Just some water."

"Okay, take your clothes off, handsome, get comfortable."

I took off my clothes, except for my underwear, and sat on the edge of his bed. He brought me my water and sat next to me, sipped his whiskey.

"What do you do? What kind of work?" he asked. I hesitated a moment and he jumped in with: "You don't have to tell me. Or you can lie. It doesn't matter. Whatever you want."

He was hungry for conversation, lonely. He had lowered the price to ensure I'd come over. I think he must have been drinking hard these last three years.

"I'm an actor," I said.

"You're in the arts," he said. "I love the arts. I wanted to be an artist."

I didn't say anything.

"I took a painting class in college," he continued; he was tipsy, slurring. "I loved it. I wanted to be a painter. I'd stay up all night painting. But this teacher, my first teacher, told me I was no good. He said I should be a hairdresser. I guess he could tell I was gay. It crushed me. I never recovered. But he was right. I was mediocre at best. You have to be great to be an artist. But I love creative things. Opera. Books. Movies. Paintings. I was in flowers. I might do it again. It's never too late. You never know."

"That wasn't fair of that teacher," I said.

"It wasn't meant to be," he said. He was full of clichés, but his story was heartbreaking.

Then he patted my knee. "Okay, good-looking."

He opened his robe. I got on my knees while he sat on the bed. I don't know why but this time I took the thing in my mouth without a condom. His big belly was just above me. I took my penis out of my boxer shorts and touched myself while he grew in my mouth. Again, I didn't get hard and I came almost immediately, maybe a minute after I had started. It was on the carpet. I stopped sucking him and we looked at the little drops on the floor.

"Don't worry about it," he said.

He went and got a paper towel and cleaned it up, which was nice of him, not asking me to do it. He put his robe back on and I started getting dressed. He watched me. He didn't ask but I put the money on his desk. I put a hundred and fifty there. He'd count it after I left.

He hugged me good-bye. He smelled of the whiskey. "I like you," he said. "Don't be a stranger."

I raced down the stairs and went to a deli across the street. I bought a small bottle of green Listerine and then in the shadows of a doorway poured a bunch of it into my mouth and then spit. I repeated this several times, until I had used up the whole bottle. People walked past me as I spit out this green water but I didn't care. I had to make sure I killed all the germs. I did worry about him looking out the window and seeing me and feeling hurt, but I thought it was unlikely that he would spot me.

I got a cab and went home. That was two years ago. I have a feeling that he is dead. Probably from drinking. But he was a nice guy. I wish that teacher hadn't crushed him.

Open City, 2008

I Played a Man Sitting on a Bench with a Beautiful Woman

She was a journalist, assigned to interview me. One of my books was coming out in her country. We met at a restaurant here in Brooklyn at five o'clock. We sat at a table on the sidewalk. It was late May, beautiful weather. She was beautiful. She had thin, elegant arms that I wanted to grab.

She also had green eyes, a misaligned front tooth, dark brown hair pulled back, a full ass, nice legs, a long nose, a thin face, a lovely neck. She was about five-six, almost tall for a woman, and she wore a yellow skirt, a white blouse, and tan sandals with a bit of heel. The blouse had maybe come undone by one button too many. Not that I minded. I caught a glimpse of a fragile white bra.

Her English was flawed but charming. She was from the capital, ——, working for her country's most famous magazine. It was a six-month assignment, covering New York, and she was heading home soon. I was one of her last profiles. My novel was coming out in June, two years after its publication here in the States. We talked about the book for an hour. She had two glasses of white wine. I had a cappuccino. I don't know if it was the coffee, but I felt something in my chest, a tightening of sorts. I'm half dead inside, but I had the thought: *Have I fallen immediately in love?*

There was nothing more to say about the book. She put her little European notepad away.

"Want to go for a walk?" I said, not wanting to lose her yet. "The light is so beautiful right now."

"Yes," she said. There was a slight husky quality to her voice and something sibilant, probably because of the front tooth.

We walked and I bored her with conversation about Brooklyn, then I said, hoping to rally, "I don't know anyone who lives in Manhattan anymore. Manhattan is the new Queens."

It was a stupid remark, one I had used before, an attempt at wit, but she didn't quite get the real estate humor. I'm not sure I get it. She said, "I'm going to miss New York. I love it. The lunacy. There's no lunacy in my country."

Lunacy must be a word that is common in her language and I admired her use of it, and love sounded like "loave." I looked at her neck. It was a beautiful neck.

She lit a cigarette. We walked slowly, and we didn't talk. It was nice to just be in the perfect light and the perfect air. She was twenty-eight but a woman. I'm forty-two but I'm a boy. I don't feel like a man. It comes from being an American and being a writer. I've never had money. Living half broke for twenty years retards your growth. You're never quite yourself. You're always waiting to grow into your life, but you never do.

And there's something about the American character that also keeps you from maturity. I don't know why this is, but it feels true.

We went to a little park. Sat on a bench. There was some grass and trees with white flowers, and mothers with children, a last bit of playing, and there was that end-of-the-day light that even in the twenty-first century makes you think the world is all right. So I played a man sitting on a bench with a beautiful woman.

"Thank you for walking with me," I said.

"I liked our walk," she said. She was sitting very close to me. I shifted on the bench and put my hand into her lush hair at the top of her neck, and then taking her hair in my hand, I turned her toward me. She completed the turn and looked at me with those green eyes. I saw shock and acquiescence, and then I kissed her.

Our lips met right and then her mouth opened and she tasted of wine and cigarettes and something sweet and it was a beautiful kiss. We kept at it. She crawled on my lap and I buried my face in her neck and then kissed her in the opening of her blouse, smelling delicious perfume. We kissed again, hard. Then we parted. We looked around. There was a child crying, having fallen. A little girl in a little dress. A beautiful child. I thought of her growing up and sitting on a man's lap on a bench. The mother gathered up the child. The journalist said, "I want to go to your apartment."

She put her arm through mine and we walked to my apartment, hardly talking, but stopping twice to kiss and for me to pull her tight against me. I'm six foot and she folded into me nicely, perfectly.

We got to my apartment, with its poor, secondhand furniture and the books on the floor. I don't have a couch, only chairs, since I'm a stunted person, and so we lay on my bed and kissed for a while, until I undressed her and then me. And I was standing by the bed, having just removed my pants, and she got off the bed and kneeled on my pants and took me in her mouth. She luxuriated in it, rubbing it against her face when it was wet and slick. She was moaning, but I started feeling selfish, so I lifted her onto the bed and sucked on her breasts. She was almost all nipple and I loved it.

Then I kissed her stomach and kept on kissing, until I put my tongue in her and there wasn't much taste but enough, salty and maddening. I put a finger inside her and felt some kind of birth-control object. I didn't want to jar it, so I took my finger out. At some point she shifted to her side and my head was encased between her legs and I stayed there and she came twice.

She pulled me up to kiss her and she started guiding me into her and I said, "I have condoms," and she said, "I have a thing," and I didn't tell her I knew, I didn't know if it was bad etiquette to say I had felt it, and so she guided me into her and it had been years since I'd had sex without a condom and it was a revelation. With a condom, after about fifteen or twenty minutes, it's like my cock goes numb, the base of the condom like a tourniquet, so I have to come at that point or suffer the mortal embarrassment of losing my erection. That said, I'm not one of those guys who's against condoms, I don't mind them too much, twenty minutes is more than enough, but this sex without the condom was like heaven.

We went at it slow. Sometimes hard. I would stop and go down on her some more. We might just lie there for a bit, holding each other and kissing, and then start the fucking again. Missionary position, she would bury her face in my shoulder and whimper quietly—she wasn't a woman who screamed, except at the end when she would come. She was very flexible and we put her legs— her knees—all the way by her head and I went in her so deep and leaned down and kissed her deep, too. She was beautiful and vulnerable.

She got on her belly and put her incredible full ass into the air and I took her that way. She got on top of me and her hair fell across her breasts, and I sat up and moved the hair and sucked on her fat nipples. She'd looked at me, grinding against me, impaled on me, and her eyes seemed to say, "I will never know you," but all eyes say that, if I think about it.

We just kept doing it and she kept coming, and oddly I never felt that thing inside her, though I had touched it with my finger. Anyway, the whole thing was astounding to me because I just kept going. Ever since I turned forty, some kind of switch went off or on, and so the gods only give me one hard-on in an evening, maybe two, whereas when I was younger I could come three or four or even five times in a night, so I've learned to make the one bullet I'm given last, but this night with the journalist was something beyond extraordinary. We had started in a dim yellow light in my room, the last bit of sun coming through the curtains, until we were in a silvery darkness, the metallic light from the streetlamps allowing me to still see her beautiful body. So we had begun making love around seven and didn't stop until almost eleven, when she told me to come in her mouth, something I usually don't like to do, I feel bad for the woman, but she wanted it and I allowed myself to believe it was okay and so then we were done, and we lay there, both of us rather unbelieving.

Then she started laughing, her laugh was husky like her voice, and she said, "Now let's talk about your cock." And cock sounded like "cawk" and it was all so bawdy in the most appealing way, just her saying the word "cock," and so I said, "What about it?" "I love it," she said, and love was "loave," and, of course, as a preening male, I was deeply pleased.

She didn't spend the night. She had a roommate from her country who knew her boyfriend back home and so she couldn't possibly return to her apartment in the morning. The roommate might say something. This came out at the end. A boyfriend back home.

So I called a car for her. I saw her again a week later and we were both aware of making it as good as that first night but it wasn't. A week after that we tried again and once more it fell short. Each time we seemed to grow more shy with each other. Then she left New York. Her article ran and was sent to me by my publisher. But I don't speak a word of her language and so I have no idea what she said.

Nerve, 2007

NEXT-DOOR NEIGHBORLESS

A TRUE STORY by Jonathan Ames & Nick Bertozzi

IN 1998, I WAS LIVING IN THE EAST VILLAGE ON THIRD STREET. I HAD ONE OF THOSE OLD-FASHIONED APARTMENTS WITH A TUB IN THE KITCHEN.

I WAS THIRTY-FOUR YEARS OLD AND MY HAIR WAS THINNING. I HAD BOUGHT A RUBBER SCALP-INVIGORATOR, WHICH I WAS TOLD MIGHT HELP RESTORE MY HAIR.

EVERY DAY I INVIGORATED MY SCALP FOR FIVE MINUTES WHILE BATHING.

THIS ONE DAY AS I WORKED ON MYSELF WITH THE INVIGORATOR, I SAW SOMETHING DOWN BY MY FEET.

IT'S A BIT EMBARASSING, BUT I THOUGHT THE DARK THING WAS SOME BLOODY SNOT THAT I HAD SHOT OUT OF MY NOSE, SO I IGNORED IT AND JUST HOPED THAT THE SNOT WOULDN'T GET STUCK IN MY LEG HAIR.

THEN THE DARK THING MOVED IN A WAY THAT DIDN'T SEEM CAPABLE FOR A PIECE OF MUCUS.

I PANICKED. THE DARK THING WAS A COCKROACH SWIMMING IN MY TUB. I FLASHED TO THOSE FISH IN THE AMAZON THAT SWIM UP A PERSON'S PENIS AND EAT IT FROM THE INSIDE.

THE WORD **COCKROACH** ONLY ADDED TO THIS MOMENTARY, IRRATIONAL FEAR.

I HAD TO PUT MY HAND IN THE WATER TO REMOVE THE PLUG SO THAT THE COCKROACH WOULD GO DOWN THE DRAIN WITH THE WATER.

I WAS SCARED TO DO THIS, BUT I SUMMONED UP THE COURAGE, THOUGH I KEPT SCREAMING OUT, INANELY, FOR HELP.

I FELT BAD DROWNING THE COCKROACH; HE DIDN'T DESERVE TO DIE, BUT IT WAS EITHER HIM OR ME.

I THOUGHT MAYBE ONE OF MY NEIGHBORS MIGHT HAVE HEARD MY CRIES FOR HELP AND COME TO MY RESCUE, BUT THERE WAS NO RESPONSE.

I FELT A LITTLE HURT BY THIS, BUT SHOOK IT OFF.

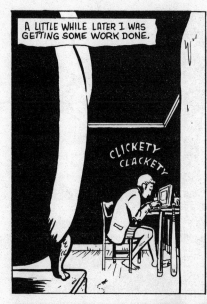

A LITTLE WHILE LATER I WAS GETTING SOME WORK DONE.

CLICKETY CLACKETY

I COULDN'T BELIEVE IT—THERE WAS ANOTHER COCKROACH.

CLAC--

I WONDERED IF IT WAS A RELATIVE OF THE COCKROACH I HAD DROWNED.

IT WAS COMING RIGHT AT ME, PERHAPS TO SEEK REVENGE.

SMITH Magazine, 2008

Acknowledgments

I would like to thank Rosalie Siegel and Brant Rumble for helping put this book together, and Doug Brod, Dave Eggers, and Tom Beller for generously publishing my work.